P R

THE GIRL WHO O

"This modern feminist folktale hides dark themes within a deceptively whimsical exterior...the engaging plot will draw readers in."

PUBLISHERS WEEKLY

"Zoje Stage has crafted the perfect fairy tale: Magical, brutal, and full of heart. A beautifully written story that I can't stop thinking about."

SAMANTHA DOWNING, internationally bestselling author of
My Lovely Wife and *For Your Own Good*

"A perfect blend of *The Wizard of Oz* meets Jerzy Kosinski, *The Girl Who Outgrew the World* reminds us of the parts of childhood too painful to remember, the people around us, who kept us small. But this time the story's rewritten: at last, it's the girl who gets to go on an epic hero's journey. Fabulous in every sense of the word."

SARAH LANGAN, author of *Good Neighbors*

"A strikingly beautiful novella about girlhood, teeming with fairy tale whimsy and heart-wrenching truth. Stage has created an entrancing, bittersweet adventure for the ages."

RACHEL HARRISON, author of *The Return* and *Cackle*

"I could feel my heart beat gold, my eyes fill with stars, and birds flutter from my mouth as I read this heart-tugging modern fairy tale. In *The Girl Who Outgrew the World*, Zoje Stage spins an enchanting modern parable in which all we hope is to be accepted as our very unique selves in this world."

CYNTHIA PELAYO, three time Bram Stoker Award-nominated author

"I cannot put into words how much I loved this book. Stage's writing is haunting and engaging, a power-punch of metaphors that transcend the words on the page...When I say this is one of the best books I've read all year, I am screaming it with my whole heart."

MANDY MCHUGH, author of *Chloe Cates is Missing*

THE
GIRL
WHO
OUTGREW
THE
WORLD

THE
GIRL
WHO
OUTGREW
THE
WORLD

ZOJE
STAGE

Published in 2022 by Lethe Press
www.lethepressbooks.com • lethepress@aol.com

Cover design and layout by JeremyJohnParker.com
Cover images by Mehdi Sepehri | unsplash.com & Deagreez | Adobe Stock

ISBN: 978-1-59021-523-4

For all the girls and women
who are ogled but overlooked,
underestimated,
disbelieved, dismissed.
Rear up like the dynamic queen
you have every right to be.
Whisper your truth
and know you are heard.

THE VILLAGE OF WRONG THINGS

The cat with two tails
  and the fish with no scales

The ghost with no scare
  and the three-headed bear

The king with no gold
  who would never grow old

The bat with no wings
  and the dragon who sings

The girl with six eyes
  and the goat who eats flies

The bird who chirps bells
  and the witch with no spells

Together they live in a town that may roam
  picking up strangers and bringing them home

—Unknown, circa 1800's

JAMES

He fought the urge to turn off the lamp and sit in the dark. Everything else was dark. The TV. The kitchen. The hallway. The street of tidy but modest homes beyond the bay window. The world had silenced itself, snuffed out the cars, muted the crickets, drawn an invisible zipper across the lips of his neighbors—as Lilly used to do, when she wanted him to promise to keep her secrets.

He longed to turn the lamp off and sit in the dark. But didn't, because that was something desperate people did in the twilight of their defeat.

His fear was unforgiveable, a betrayal worse than any misdeed of his thirty-four years. He was afraid of Lilly. Afraid that she was fundamentally something...*else*. In spite of his efforts to affix his apple-of-my-eye smile of approval, more and more it dribbled off like milk over the edge of a table. Somewhere on the floor were a thousand quivering mouths. Worse, he saw his rejection in his daughter's eyes. His hesitation. The mourned loss of their physical language of hugs and squeezes. Even ordinary words had become too fragile to hold. In the absence of an explanation there was only the obvious: unknowable and slack-jawed. It stank of danger. Of something primordial he couldn't comprehend.

Eight weeks ago they'd cuddled in this very chair, her legs draped across his lap; they'd watched her favorite show about a girl who could fly. She was too big for that now. The chair too small. When the growth spurt first started Lilly crowed her delight. She'd been nervous about starting sixth grade and a bit more height—"a more impressive stature"— gave her confidence. But by the time school started, barely three weeks ago, Lilly was taller than the teachers. Taller than her father.

Lilly once asked, her voice seesawing between horror and awe, "Daddy, am I a monster?"

And he said "No no, just a friendly giant."

That was mid-August, when she went from four foot nine to five foot seven and her height still seemed within the realm of possibility. They bantered about the new sports she could try. Volleyball. Water polo.

But Lilly kept growing and the doctor stopped joking about the healthy effects of the summer sun. A weed. A stalk of corn.

James surrendered and switched off the lamp, afraid his daughter would stumble in needing a drink of water or another Tylenol—her eleven-year-old bones *hurt*—before falling asleep. Sometimes she forgot to duck and hit her head on the doorjamb. It pained him to see it. He wondered if she was right.

A monster.

Unsure what to do, he shut his eyes.

LILLY

Her feet hung over the end of the bed. Daddy promised her a big bed—and a new wardrobe—once they were certain the growth spurt had stopped. Not long ago her bedroom had been a favorite place. Now, the stuffed toys were too small to hug and the dollhouse miniatures were like slippery peanuts in her clumsy hands. The top of her bookcase hid a layer of dust which she otherwise wouldn't have seen. Instead of cleaning it, she'd used a finger to spell out her name.

Her exposed toes grew cold in the dark.

The dark bred the doubts that crept toward her throat, threatening to strangle her.

She had never wished for a mommy before—Daddy's love was an endless ocean. (Though oceans weren't truly endless, but they were vast, and deep, and the birthplace of all living things.) Even when Lilly grew distressed—"it's my fault"—because Mommy died while giving birth to her, Daddy always said "No no, you are the gift that keeps on giving." But now...

In the dark of her bedroom...

As her knees hummed like the deep bass of a loud song...

She hoped she wasn't being disloyal just to wonder, to ponder the possibility that a mommy might find a better temporary solution than the Big & Tall Men's Store, or men's basketball shoes. Maybe a mommy would sew her a sundress out of a pretty fabric shower curtain. And shopping for a bra with a mommy wouldn't be weird. Lilly hadn't needed a bra before, but the whole of her had grown exponentially (minus some bits and pieces). Her little buds were now small boobs; at least they weren't as out of proportion as her hands and nose.

As Lilly turned over to get more comfortable, her thick hips dug into the thin mattress. Maybe a mommy wouldn't be as afraid of her as a daddy. Maybe a mommy would say "Girls grow buttercup, suck it up" to anyone with a questioning gaze. She understood some of Daddy's fears: What if she outgrew their house? What if she outgrew the world? But she hadn't yet, and while she'd never given much thought to the variables of human size, she knew she wasn't beyond being a person—though she was beyond the accepted norms for a girl.

JAMES

Every morning James eyed her as she came into the kitchen, trying to gauge if she was any taller. Her hair didn't look clean—she wasn't used to the handheld nozzle and inevitably sprayed water around the bathroom as her elbows collided with the narrow walls of the shower stall. But Lilly hadn't noticeably grown in a week.

Maybe it was time to make good on his promise and get her out of those men's chinos, the stuffy buttoned shirt that made his little girl—if he could still call her that—look more like an insurance salesman than a middle school student. Lilly once had long hair and she'd proudly worn it in two braids that she'd woven herself. As she gained her height, her hair hadn't kept up. It swung unhappily above her shoulders now, almost too short for Lilly to hide behind. Her fingernails, also, hadn't grown proportionately, which made her hands look grotesque, paws with dull splinters of moon.

She gripped her fork, her tongue poking from between her lips, and watched with the attention of a bloodthirsty hunter as he slid the dozen scrambled eggs onto her plate.

"Thanks, Daddy." Her voice was still that of a small

child. If he hadn't seen her mouth move it might have been a ventriloquist's trick, throwing the voice of a girl who no longer existed.

"Did you sleep well?" He returned the skillet to the stove, nibbling on the remnants.

Lilly shrugged, chewed. "Not really."

His expression softened as he studied her. It wasn't her fault, any of it. And it hurt her. Physically, and in ways he couldn't imagine. She needed something from him and he didn't know what to offer.

"We can ask the doctor about it on Friday." They went to the doctor's every week now, to monitor and theorize.

Lilly shrugged again. It struck him how resigned she was: this was her new body, her new life. Her growth couldn't be undone. The doctor had been straightforward about that, back when they were looking for a pituitary tumor. Then the scan came back negative. Specialists were consulted. They sat in a conference room at the hospital, a half dozen doctors projected like game show contestants on a big screen, asking questions, comparing research. No one knew anything.

"We'll make her as comfortable as possible," Lilly's pediatrician had whispered to him. They thought she was going to die. They thought she would grow until her heart burst.

"I think...Everything fits the same," he said, inspecting her, lingering over the small bulges on her chest, a development that ruled out gigantism, which typically caused a delay in puberty not an acceleration. "Your shoes still okay?"

"Yup. It's been a whole week!"

He didn't know if she understood. The possibility of what could happen if she kept growing.

"Maybe we should hire that seamstress." He threw her a wink.

"Really?" Her grin made a clownish face, with her nose wide and taut, but her delight was undeniable.

James decided then and there: even if his little girl kept growing—grew beyond the logistics of a coffin—he'd get a whole team of seamstresses on the job that very day.

James drove her to school, as had become their routine. It was close enough to walk and Lilly seemed unaware that everyone stared when they saw her. People weren't unkind—it was almost as if they saw the reaper in her shadow, waiting to carry her off to the netherworld the instant she crossed some invisible boundary. They had pity in their eyes, but also terror—that such a random wrongness might befall them or someone they knew. It was James who didn't like the spectacle of it.

As he braked in front of the squat one-story middle school, Lilly unfolded herself from the front seat—pushed all the way back to make room for her. Like a magical creation of origami, she angled herself out of the car, a paper doll whose limbs, uncrimped, expanded upward. She didn't lean in to kiss him goodbye anymore because it hurt her back, but James threw her kisses and reminded her of his promise. The army of seamstresses. The new and beautiful wardrobe.

She strode up the walkway, the smile on her face visible even from behind. He watched as she greeted a friend—bless her friends, the smart and giggly girls who still accepted Lilly just as she was—and tried not to notice the slight limp in her walk. Whether her gait was uneven because of lingering pain or because her legs were now slightly mismatched, James wasn't sure. But, like so many things since Lilly's affliction began, it ravaged him like he'd swallowed a grenade.

One hand on the door, Lilly turned to wave at him, still abloom with the promise of the return of her skirts and colors and mismatched plaids and polka dots that expressed her whimsy, her confident I-am-who-I-am. She ducked and followed her friends inside. Maybe it was those plaids and polka dots that had prepared her for this—for being a standout in their small community of green lawns, everyone decapitated by the same ruthless lawnmower.

He was an Eye-Tea man. When Lilly was little she'd peer into his coffee mug, on the lookout for floating eyeballs, until she finally understood what IT meant. It was the perfect at-home career for the single father. After Daphne's unexpected death, his guilt-ridden parents had helped him acquire a small house, and there he and his daughter lived, worked, and played. It was a more enclosed life than he'd expected, but Lilly the Light always kept him from mourning. She was the best sun a father could have—a joke that confused people who thought he meant a *son*.

A cloud moved over the house.

The room instantly darkened, as if there'd been an eclipse.

The furniture faded into the background—the wide

desk, the ergonomic chair, the hard drives and cables—as his computer's triple screens luminesced. He'd already researched local tailors, and there was only one good option: Kendra's Kustomwear. Her specialties included prom dresses, maternity clothes, and tailoring for Little People. Lilly wasn't pregnant or a dwarf, and she didn't need a glittery dress, but the combined expertise in the oddly-sized and feminine sounded promising. He tapped in the number.

"Kendra's Kustomwear, Kendra speaking, how may I help you?" She answered on the second ring and spoke with a slight southern twang.

"Hello, my name is James Wolf. I'm looking for someone who could make a complete wardrobe for my daughter. You see, Lilly—"

"The little girl who grew?"

"Excuse me?"

"Isn't she the girl who grew so suddenly this summer? I was hoping you'd call me—I wanted to reach out, but I didn't want to impose."

Of course he knew Lilly wasn't a secret. Such things were impossible in the age of cellphones and the internet, and he'd even allowed a piece to be written about her for a scientific magazine, hoping to elicit answers from distant doctors or researchers.

"Yes, Lilly—"

"Oh Mr. Wolf, I can't tell you how glad I am you called! My church has been praying for your little girl. And I'd be happy to make her whatever she needs."

In spite of the discomfort he felt that a stranger was so aware of his predicament, he was also relieved. He'd dreaded trying to answer "What size does she wear?"

"I'm sorry to impose like this," he said, "but every-thing's happened so quickly and she's been wearing men's clothes. I'd really like to get her back into something more age appropriate as soon—"

"Of course! No woman—or little girl—wants to be stuck wearing fashions that don't suit her, we all want to look pretty, don't we?"

James wasn't sure how to answer that. Looking pretty had never been a major concern for him. "Can you give me an estimate? Do you charge by the piece, the hour?"

"Don't worry, Mr. Wolf. I know you have a lot more to worry about than the price of girls' underthings. My church has been gathering donations for you and we'll put it toward the cost of fabric, and I have a crew of volunteer sewers who help me when we're making things for the overseas orphan-ages and whatnot. We're always ready for a mission! We'll get your daughter feeling good about herself again in no time." She sounded as buoyant as a balloon.

He deleted his most uncharitable thought—that Kend-ra was a Kook, a Do-Gooder with Jesus on one shoulder and a beauty pageant trophy on the other. Her priorities seemed a bit off. Unless they weren't. Was Lilly feeling bad about herself? She couldn't see much in the bathroom mirror any-more, but was all of this taking a toll on her self-esteem? He'd learned from the mommy blogs how susceptible girls were to basing their self-worth on their physical appearance, so he'd always made sure to praise Lilly for meaningful things: her brains, her creativity, her hard work and kindness.

As if he wasn't a complete hypocrite. Half-worried by her changing body, half-disgusted.

Had he forgotten to compliment her in recent weeks?

It was getting harder and harder to even look at her. Even when she wasn't shoveling a week's worth of food in her mouth, she was always on display: a misshapen troll who'd taken up residence in their gingerbread house.

"How soon can you start?" he asked.

They arranged for Kendra to come over at five. James thanked her and couldn't get off the phone fast enough. Something about the transaction made him feel like a failure. Kendra acted like she knew the whole story, but what did she really *think*? Freak show? Charity case? James hoped he wasn't making a mistake, inviting someone into his home whose motivation might be to snoop more than it was to help.

Kendra's konfidence—and her unnamed sources of information—piqued his curiosity about what else was out there. He'd intended to spend part of his day trying to dig up more medical theories, even remote ones that only people who believed in extraterrestrial visitation might accept. But instead he Googled "Lilly Wolf." And "giant girl." And slipped down the rabbit hole of cyber gossip.

LILLY

illy had her own table at the back of the social studies class. And a hard wooden chair that swiveled and squeaked but was a solid as a tank circa World War I. Many of the rooms now had a similar set up, a necessary accommodation for Lilly's Unusual Stature. At first she'd objected to her exile at the back of the class, but now she rather liked the view and thought of herself as a periscope, keeping an eye on everything that bobbed in the water. Her best friend Rain was always allowed to sit beside her, which made a lot of things about middle school and being a giant rather better than expected.

Ms. Molina, a young teacher who somehow managed to seem exuberant and laid back at the same time, half-leaned, half-sat on the front of her desk, ankles and wrists delicately crossed as she waited for someone other than Lilly to raise a hand. It wasn't that Ms. Molina wouldn't call on her—quite the opposite—but she always paused to see if anyone else wanted to participate.

Her classmates' behavior, especially the girls, puzzled Lilly. Where last year they'd been quick to give an answer or eager to ask a question, they'd lost their voices over the summer. Lilly imagined them at the same overnight camp-of-horrors, where their personalities had been extracted with a slender hook that went up a nostril and pulled out a sticky portion of their Silly Putty brains. The Egyptians had used such a process to make mummies, but her class-mates were zombies now, with well-manicured hands. Hands they rarely opted to raise. A scent of fear clung to them, though what clung to the boys was more like bore-dom, or the dirt of indifference.

"Lilly?" Ms. Molina smiled at her, an expression more sad than happy. It was a look Lilly was seeing more often on the adults she encountered, and if it held an undercur-rent of what-is-going-to-become-of-you, Lilly opted not to notice. She hadn't firmly decided how she felt about her new self, but she retained enough hope not to assume the worst.

"Hatshepsut!" She might've pronounced it wrong, but she'd loved reading about the first woman pharaoh.

"And the significance of her reign was...?"

"People thought she would just be regent until her stepson was old enough, but her reign was so successful that she never stepped down." A conspiratorial grin trav-eled from Lilly to Rain, Lilly to Ms. Molina—some secret understanding that taking over the world was the right thing for girls to do.

As if sensing a threat, a hand shot up from the mid-dle of the room, belonging to a pudgy-cheeked boy whose name Lilly always forgot. Bryce or Bruce or Brace. He didn't wait for Ms. Molina's permission to blurt out, "Shouldn't she be in college? It isn't fair."

Rain mouthed "college?" and she and Lilly snorted

before giggling behind their hands.

Bruce or Brace or Bryce whipped around to scowl at them.

"Lilly knows the answer because she read the—"

Before Ms. Molina could finish, and heedless of his own folly, Brace or Bryce or Bruce interrupted her. "There's no way she's a sixth grader, she might not even be a girl. No one that big can—"

This time it was Rain who took offense. "You think tall people can't be young, or girls? That's the dumbest—"

"Okay, let's—" Ms. Molina shifted away from her desk and onto her feet.

"My brain is a lot bigger now," Lilly said in her own defense. "So I guess you're right, that might be a little unfair."

Half the class, already amused by the departure from their regular routine, roared their approval; none of them returned with a litter to carry the now pink-cheeked boy from the battlefield. And whatever admonishment Ms. Molina had been on the verge of unleashing to settle the matter, instead she pressed her lips together to keep from looking too amused. But Lilly saw the glint of approval in her eyes.

After school, Lilly and Rain walked to Rain's house; Lilly was glad to stretch out her legs. Sometimes, as she and her best friend gabbled about the who and what of their day, Lilly missed seeing a low-hanging branch before it struck her in the face. Rain chided her as if she'd always been so tall, always forgetting to move tree limbs out of the way because of her love for leaf sandwiches.

"...and much smaller than a bee, but quite larger than a flea..." The high-pitched voice came from above.

The girls looked around to see which bird had spoken. Most people considered the birds and their anthropomorphic chatter a nuisance, but Lilly had an affinity for them. Some sang the ditties from radio commercials, and some imitated the people they heard. Some had such mysterious things to say, a riddle, or a fragment of heartfelt advice. A few even sounded like other animals, the croaking frog, the meowing cat, the midnight cricket.

"...that would be the ladybird, the ladybug another word." It was the little brown bird with the white stripes on its wings, reciting in a grandmotherly tone. Lilly grinned, eager to hear the rest of the poem, but her head came too near the bird's nest and it flew away.

By the time they arrived at Rain's house Lilly had acquired a few scratches—on her forehead, on her left cheek—but was otherwise not worse for the wear.

"Snack?" Rain asked as she tossed her backpack onto the kitchen's cluttered island.

"I'm starving!" Lilly sat on one of the wooden bar stools and shoved away a pile of mail, a menagerie of pens, a flashlight, and two screwdrivers, until she had enough space to rest her elbows.

"Chips and salsa? PB&J?"

"Sure."

"Which?" The light from the refrigerator lit up Rain's face and cast a sheen on her curtain of black hair. They used to take turns braiding each other's hair and Lilly had loved the comfort of her friend's fingers twisting and stroking her long locks. It was the thing she'd become most self-conscious about, her hair a noticeable deficit where everything else—legs, nose, boobs, hands—were on the scale of abundance, even if in excess.

"Both? I'm really hungry."

Rain handed over the bag of tortilla chips and jar of salsa. "We've got more if you finish that."

"Thanks." If Lilly hadn't been so hungry she would've helped make the sandwiches, but over the past weeks an unspoken arrangement had settled into their friendship: Rain helped whenever she could. She didn't ask or make a big deal of it, she just picked up whatever Lilly dropped, held doors open, tied her sneakers if they came undone. Sometimes she knew Lilly needed assistance before Lilly realized it herself, like when they made the year's first poster project and Rain automatically trimmed all the pictures they'd printed: Lilly couldn't use scissors anymore, the finger holes were too small.

The phone rang.

"Probably my mom," Rain said as she spread plum jam on a slice of bread.

Lilly dug out the cordless handset from the detritus in front of her. Recognizing the caller, she answered it. "Hi Daddy."

Rain turned to her, grinning. It was a running wish between them that their loving and well-meaning parents either left them alone, or got them their own damn phones. The adults were in cahoots about the evils of cellular phone dependency: The isolating tendency to ignore everything except the small glowing screen; the perilous access to social media—where they might attract bullies or perverts. Rain's brother Declan just got his cellphone a few weeks ago, when he started high school. The girls still hoped not to wait that long.

"Good..." Lilly gobbled tortilla chips, heavily laden with spicy tomatillo salsa, as they went through their usual after-school convo. "No, not really...A little..." Her dad finally said something that sparked her interest. Lilly's eyes widened and she perked up. "Really?...Can Rain come over?... Okay, bye!"

Rain slid their two plates onto the island, pushing away more stuff, and sat on the stool beside Lilly. "What's up?"

"My dad's picking me up at four-forty-five because guess what? He found a lady who makes custom clothes and she's coming over at five to start working on my—"

"Holy galoshes, that's so awesome! Can you design anything you want?"

"I think so. Want to come over and help me—" A crack like a bat hitting a ball startled them out of their conversation. The next thing Lilly knew she was sitting on the tiled floor, the stool in splintered fragments around her.

"Are you okay?" Rain leapt onto the floor beside Lilly.

Everything in her vision wobbled for a minute. Lilly wasn't sure if she was okay. The core of her body ached as her spine shouted in protest at being unceremoniously dumped on the ground.

"Lilly? Are you hurt? Should I call your dad?"

"No, I'm okay, just...Wasn't expecting that. Sorry." What Lilly felt most was embarrassment. Had her weight weakened the stool in recent weeks? Should she have known it couldn't hold her anymore? "I'll buy you a new one," she mumbled.

"Who cares, it's just an ancient dumb chair." Rain

stood, gripping her friend's arm, prepared to help her up. But Lilly wasn't quite ready.

"Will your parents be mad?"

Rain just gave her a look, a don't-be-ridiculous, a look-at-the-state-of-our-house, a you've-known-my-parents-forever look, which made Lilly feel a little better. But just a little.

"What if I outgrow the world?"

"Oh Lilly." Rain embraced her, crouching so Lilly could weep on her shoulder. "It'll be okay."

"Sometimes I don't mind it, but sometimes...What if I never stop?"

"You will."

It's what everyone said—her grandparents, the nurses, the scan technicians, teachers, Rain's parents—because it *should* be true. A person shouldn't be able to keep growing forever. But nothing about Lilly's growth spurt conformed to the known rules of being human. And sometimes, when the consequences lay in pieces all around her, it made her worried. And a little scared.

She planted one hand on the tile floor and her feet flat on the ground. Rain, who'd once been quite a bit taller than she, used the strength she'd acquired from years of playing soccer and helped hoist her up. Both girls grunted with the exertion of it, which turned to laughter as Lilly, fully upright, found herself just beneath the light fixture, which floated over her head like a fancy glass hat.

"It looks good on you," said Rain.

"Maybe I'll design a dress to go with it."

Rain didn't let go of her hand. "You're a superhero. Don't forget that."

Lilly heard the unshed tears in her best friend's voice.

Where once it had just been adults who were afraid for her, now Rain was too. But Lilly had a magic trick for keeping her own fear at bay: no matter what happened, she knew Rain would always be her friend.

LILLY

The basement was the hangout place though it was nicer and tidier than the Shens' living room (even with its walls painted the sweetened beige of a rotting peach). It was comfy down there, with a squishy old sofa (slightly stained), an old TV, and, other than a couple pair of Declan's shoes, a surprising lack of clutter. Lilly now had to descend the carpeted steps very carefully or her head would bonk the angled ceiling of the stairwell. But once downstairs she could stand upright, and open her arms without fear of knocking anything over.

Their sandwiches were long since gone, but Lilly kept munching on chips as they watched one of their favorite shows: a kindhearted UK import where a trio of professionals made over punks and freaks and insecure girls with ninety layers of spray tan. The stylists gently showed them how beautiful they were without all their makeup and piercings and false eyelashes. Some of the transformations were remarkable, and it gave Lilly hope that even the oddest girl could be seen as beautiful.

At the start of their second episode, Declan made his way down the stairs and plopped onto the reclining chair beside the sofa. He took off his kicks—in his size, the basketball shoes looked cool not monstrous—and threw them in the corner with the others.

"Chickadees," he said by way of hello.

"Hey."

Rain said nothing. Where she was used to her brother's presence, Lilly still felt grateful when he graced them with his company. Not only was he older and adorable, but he was also genuinely sweet. The previous year when she and Rain had to sell candy to raise money for the school choir's out-of-state performance, Declan sold half their inventory to his friends. And for Rain's ninth birthday he'd shamelessly joined them in the basement for their karaoke contest, making sure, by crooning loudly and hilariously out of tune, that he was the obvious loser.

"Rain? You down there?" The voice came from the top of the stairs.

She shot her brother a confused look. "What's she doing home?"

Usually their mom didn't come home until six. Declan shrugged, indifferent.

"Yeah?" Rain called, sounding uncertain.

"You've got an eye appointment, we need to go."

Rain and Lilly turned to each other, frowning. "I forgot," Rain whispered. To the ceiling she said, "Can we reschedule?"

"No, come on. Is Lilly there—does she need a ride home?"

"My dad will be here in a few minutes."

"Okay." And then footsteps crossed above them.

The girls gazed at her other with exaggerated regret at

their imminent separation.

"Call me later and tell me everything," Rain said as she got up.

"I will. You getting new glasses?"

"Maybe. My mom thinks I squint too much. See ya."

"Ciao."

"Later, squirt," Declan held up a hand, not quite a wave, as Rain disappeared up the stairs.

Lilly couldn't decide if having fifteen minutes alone with Declan was the greatest thing that ever happened to her, or the most awkward. She was aware of him in her peripheral vision, his mop of black hair, his grimy socks, and couldn't help but wonder what he thought of her new elongated state. Assuming her presence even registered. With her legs stretched out they filled most of the distance between the sofa and the television. But Declan had a way of appearing indifferent to everything, the solitary member of his own parallel universe.

With her eyes glued to the television (where a blue-mohawked girl in platform boots was wiping off her stripes of black eyeliner, revealing a surprisingly innocent face), Lilly weighed the pros and cons of attempting a conversation. Con: Declan might ignore her or think she was ridiculous. Pro: He might respond with something funny that would bring the warm blush of achievement to her insides, which of late had been feeling quite hollow in spite of how much she ate.

There was movement on her left as Declan pivoted, and before she could register what was happening he had decamped and was sitting on the couch beside her.

"Howdy."

She froze for a moment, unsure what to do. A part of her was afraid to look at him, but the other part didn't want to seem rude or creepy. Finally, she stopped tracking him in her peripheral vision and turned her head to meet his eyes.

"Howdy," she mimicked back, and immediately feared she sounded like a bird.

"Can I ask you something?"

"Okay." It was an unexpected development and she hoped he only wanted to make a silly inquiry and not ask one of the what-is-it-like-to-be-a-giant questions, like the kids at school.

Declan gazed at her with an intensity he usually reserved for video games and somehow his body had come so close that his knee pressed against the outside of her thigh. "Has anyone ever touched you?"

That was his question? Lilly felt the squirming eels of confusion. She'd spent a lifetime hugging people. Her dad caressed her back when she was sick or couldn't sleep. Her grandparents always gave her a loud kiss on the cheek. She and Rain gripped hands when they were especially happy or excited. It was a dumb question. She glanced at his knee, where it still rested against her leg. His eyes followed hers.

"No, I don't mean like..." Was he blushing? "I mean like real touching. Like, with a boy."

"No?" It sounded like a question, two syllables, her pitch rising at the end. What was he getting at? He couldn't possibly be interested in her—she was three years younger *and* his little sister's best friend. He was in *high school*. She wasn't an expert, but she was pretty sure most boys liked the older girls with the bigger boobs...Oh.

Could that be his interest? Her eleven-year-old body that didn't look eleven anymore?

"So would that be okay, if I...?" His hand twitched, like he wasn't sure what to do with it. He rested it on her bulbous knee, then thought better of it and moved it to his own knee. "Only if you want to. And over your shirt, not under."

Lilly had no clue what she was supposed to think about this development. Yay? Gross? It was hard to comprehend why touching a fleshy chest blob held such interest for him. She tried to imagine what it would feel like—from his perspective as well as her own—but as the silence stretched into something gummy and uncomfortable she knew she had to reply.

"Okay." Her answer lacked enthusiasm, though the more she thought about it the more curious she became.

Declan wasted no time, bouncing so close to her that his leg was almost atop hers. He put his left hand on her right breast, lightly over her ugly blouse, then cupped it a little. Lilly stared at him, trying to guess from his expression what he was feeling. He, too, seemed more curious than anything else; she couldn't feel that much through the bra's padding.

His face was just inches away and she saw black pores on his chin where he hadn't scrubbed well enough. There was a speck of orange dust in the corner of his lip and recognizing it made her aware of his Dorito breath. Gaining confidence, he squeezed a little, and made a circular motion with his hand that made her tingle in a surprising way. He gripped and groped and fondled.

"Oh!" She hadn't meant to say anything, and was almost afraid he could see, or sense, that something unusual

34

was happening to her, deep inside. She half-expected her skin to change color, take on the cobalt hue of the inner core of a flame.

"Is that okay?" Declan asked, removing his hand.

"Yes. It felt nice. I wasn't sure it would."

That made him smile. The tension eased from his body and he looked relieved. And a bit proud. He moved away from her a few inches, nodding his head.

"Don't tell anyone about this, okay? Even my sister."

"Why?" The glow she'd felt suddenly sizzled. A wisp of dark smoke curled into a question mark in the air above them, its scent an alarm.

"Well...it's just...private, you know."

It might be weird to tell Rain that her brother had touched her boob, but it would be just as weird to not tell her. They shared everything; she didn't like to think of their relationship changing, or of secrets coming between them. Especially ones that Lilly felt she had a right to share. Wasn't it her body? But then again, it was private. And perhaps, as Declan was suggesting in the hesitant spaces between his words, it was something a little bit...wrong?

Lilly wished she understood better why this brief exploratory experiment might have been wrong—was he not supposed to have touched her? was she not supposed to have enjoyed it?—but if she couldn't talk about it she'd have to figure it out for herself.

"Okay," she said softly. What they'd done wasn't sex, but maybe it was an element of sex, and maybe at eleven it was something she wasn't really allowed to do. That smoky question mark took on the aroma of a forest fire—perhaps one she had inadvertently started. Now to her confusion she added guilt. And shame. The shame alone would keep her from telling anyone.

"Okay, cool." He seemed like a regular doofus again as he leaned back and re-engaged with their TV show. The blue-mohawked girl was now a young woman with a pixie cut and a sheath dress. Her reflection in the full-length mirror looked baffled. *Is that me?* Lilly knew just how she felt—all new on the outside while inside she was the same. "She's hot," said Declan.

Lilly got up to leave. Might as well wait for her dad outside, where she could be alone with her thoughts and her body parts. Something had betrayed her but she wasn't sure what.

"Lilly?"

She stopped just as she reached the steps.

"Be careful. With boys. Okay?"

Were they dangerous? She wanted to ask, but didn't want to sound naïve. "Okay."

Muddled, she lowered her head and climbed the stairs.

JAMES

The doubt that had started as a sapling in midsummer had since found purchase in the fertile soil of his gloomy intestines. As the days passed it grew wildly, like Lilly, developing roots and branches and solidifying his sense of having lost control of fatherhood. Now he relished all the more the simple chores of preparing the façade, the orderly appearance of a home where nothing was overtly amiss. He didn't understand why other men shirked their domestic tasks when they were the clearest evidence of being a capable, caring provider. He'd already vacuumed the living room in preparation for Kendra's arrival, and now slid a lasagna into the oven.

Lilly sat on the sofa with her math book, though her fidgety foot and pencil tapping betrayed her lack of concentration. The doorbell rang and she sprang up. James caught his breath; soon she would be in danger of denting the ceiling—hurting herself—by such an outburst of excitement. Fearing how the sight of Lilly looming in the doorway might overwhelm their guest, he hurried to let her in himself.

"Kendra, hi—thank you so much for coming." He was amazed by how well she matched the image he'd formed in his head. Pear-shaped; colorful; coffee hair neatly coiffed; nails sharp and shiny pink. She carried the strong scent of a flowering garden.

"My pleasure! Sorry I'm a few minutes late." Her bags, one over each shoulder, were stuffed with neatly rolled fabric samples and binders bulging with swatches and patterns. "And you must be Lilly!"

Of course, the towering, grinning girl was his daughter.

"Hi!" Lilly was aglow, and James was relieved that Kendra hadn't missed a beat, hadn't reacted in any way that indicated shock or judgement.

"I am so glad to make your acquaintance, sweetheart—now where should we set up shop?"

As James guided her in, Lilly scooped up her schoolbooks and backpack, diminutive on her frame, and quickly ferried everything to her room. The seamstress took over the couch and started laying out fabrics. The second Lilly returned she knelt on the floor, in awe of the Kendra's wares.

Kendra held up a swatch of red ripstop nylon. "This would be perfect for a new schoolbag—a backpack, or a messenger bag, whatever you like."

Lilly fingered the fabric, beaming. "Oh, I hadn't thought of that."

"You're gonna feel so much better when everything you have is proportional to *you*, it's the key to being tall or short, big-boned or small—you get the proportions right and everything just looks *good*." Lilly nearly squirmed with delight. James couldn't help but smile even as he hovered over the proceedings, still concerned that it might go sideways.

"This is just like the TV show Rain and I were watching—I wish she could've come."

"Is Rain your friend?"

"My best friend."

"Aw, that's nice, well you can surprise her with all your new garments. What should we start with, what are your must-haves?"

"Blue jeans," said Lilly.

"All her basics, socks—"

"Now what is our girl going to do about shoes?" Kendra asked, averting her gaze from the submarine-sized sneakers. "Are you getting those custom too? In other words, what types of socks will you be needing? Thick, thin? Crew length, knee socks?"

Lilly looked at her dad, eyes wide with longing. He knew she missed her glittery silver high-tops, and the flowered Mary Janes. She'd probably never wear flip-flops again (her toenails, unfortunately, matched the scab-like nails on her fingers), and would never wear high heels (with her height already so intimidating). But Kendra was right—she deserved to have something she liked, that made her feel good about herself.

"We're still working on that," he said gently, looking at his daughter, passing her a silent promise. He felt stupid. It was a lot easier to find a seamstress than a cobbler. The very word—cobbler—made him think of fairytales: puppets come to life, beanstalks, mean stepsisters, poisonous apples. If this were a fairytale, as it sometimes seemed, Lilly would meet a deformed old woman who would tell her the answers could be found if she crossed six oceans, or plucked a golden leaf from the garland of an albino giraffe. If only a solution were so simple; if only Kendra were that mythological godmother.

Realizing they were both still looking to him for direction, he rearranged his face, hoping they hadn't seen his hopelessness. "We don't need to focus on the feet first. I'm sure Kendra can make you some beautiful clothes. Should we start with shirts?"

"Oh yes—I'm sure you need quite a few shirts, and do you like skirts?" Kendra's easy manner and enthusiasm saved the day.

Lilly nodded, shifting to a more comfortable position, the shoes momentarily forgotten. "Maybe knee-length? And I need some short-sleeved shirts, and some long-sleeved for when it gets cooler. Pullover kind, and maybe some buttoned ones."

"Absolutely. And do you like hoodies?"

"I *love* hoodies! Anything with a hood. And pockets. Lots of pockets."

"What about leggings? All the girls are wearing them."

Lilly emphatically shook her head, an appalled grimace on her face. All the girls *were* wearing them and James thought they were entirely too revealing—the full silhouette of the lower female body on display for all to see. He wasn't a perv, but sometimes it was hard not to notice a particularly nice bottom or a shapely pair of legs. Or wonder about The Triangle, barely hidden by the thin stretchy fabric (there was so much variety in genitalia). Nobody needed to be looking at his daughter that way, especially at her age, and in her condition. It was a relief that Lilly thought the idea more abhorrent than he did.

"So I think our plan should be: get the jeans and a few shirts made first. And my girls and I will work on more pieces and deliver them every few days, until you have a good inventory. Does that sound good?"

Lilly nodded like mad. "That sounds amazing!"

"So I'll just have you stand up straight and I'll take a few pictures."

This was what James had been anticipating. Lilly was unaware of how many phone calls he fielded, how many emails from news outlets and gossip rags and TV talk shows, all wanting to see his daughter, The Giant. The kids at school were sneaking pictures of her—he'd seen them on the internet. The word of her existence was spreading by the day.

Lilly unfolded to her full height while Kendra opened her camera app. James jumped in between them.

"I'm sorry, I can't allow you to take Lilly's picture."

"It's just so I have a visual for my measurements."

"I'm sure, but..." He wasn't sure, and he didn't care if he was assuming the worst. Their home was going to remain a Safe Place, maybe the only place where Lilly wouldn't be leered or jeered at. Or photographed.

"Daddy?"

He probably looked insane with his arms outstretched, as if Kendra couldn't see Lilly skyscraping behind him. Kendra's mouth softened from a questioning pucker to a conciliatory smile.

"Of course, I understand—I'm sorry, I should have asked first."

"It's okay, it's just...People everywhere are taking pictures of her."

"They are?" Lilly sounded so innocent and baffled.

"Yes, Lil—it's an invasion of her privacy," he said, turning back to Kendra.

Poor Lilly still looked perplexed, but Kendra, thank goodness, tucked the phone back in her purse.

"I can only imagine. I'm sorry sweetheart, I didn't mean to be insensitive. Why don't we just take measurements the old-fashioned way and leave it at that. Will that be okay?" she asked James.

He nodded, relieved, and retreated to the kitchen entryway so Kendra could finish her work. She tucked a pencil behind her ear and took out a notepad and a measuring tape. Lilly knelt awkwardly, following the directions to hold out one arm, and then the other, as Kendra unspooled the tape from shoulder to elbow to hand, and around her wrist, around her bicep. The inch-marks stretched across her upper back and Kendra, expressionless, jotted down the numbers. When Kendra wrapped the tape around Lilly's chest the girl pinkened and tilted her face toward the ceiling. Then Lilly stood and Kendra reached around her waist, her hips. She measured each of Lilly's legs.

James felt voyeuristic, watching this necessary dance play out. Well-practiced, Kendra moved from limb to limb without preamble or apology.

When they were finished, Lilly lowered herself onto the carpeted floor. She'd always liked to sit there, leaning against the couch, though James doubted it was still comfortable for her. Lilly remained at heart a child, accustomed to the habits and tendencies of children. But if her bones kept growing, putting such demands on her circulatory system... He tried to remember how long the giants in the *Guinness Book of World Records* had lived—into their twenties? Thirties? Was his precious girl already middle-aged?

"Mm, something smells good," Kendra said as she double-checked her to-do list.

"Lasagne."

"That's nice." She flashed him a warm smile, as if aware of their limited time, the dinners he would never get to make.

Though everything she did was straightforward, James couldn't banish the fear of a hidden intent behind every gesture, every word—something that might yet come back to haunt him if he couldn't decipher this seemingly kind woman's true nature. Lilly remained blissfully unconcerned, flipping through the fabrics and identifying the ones she liked. Or perhaps what was really bothering him was the way he stood there, on the outside, not quite a participant, not quite useful. He felt that way a lot now, removed from everything, and hated the sensation that his daughter wasn't growing but disappearing. There she was, larger than life, but James saw her as if in a dream, floating off into the vacuum of space. Oblivion. Where it was cold and dark and he couldn't accompany her.

It triggered a recollection—inexplicably and regrettably—of his own childhood. The golden light of his family home. His rosy-cheeked mother who always wore hot mitts, always (in his memory) in front of the oven, pulling out fresh cookies. And his father, with his brown sensible shoes, never exhausted from a day at the office, sitting in the kitchen, reading aloud from a newspaper or book that had sparked his interest.

"Isn't that something," his father would say, amazed by the world, while James savored the melting chocolate of his mother's love.

It had all been too good; he believed that now. Maybe

in his selfish childhood he consumed the reservoir of goodness. Or maybe, as a selfish adult, he'd grown lazy, expectant, entitled. And while he was distracted by the goodness of his own past, the darkness snuck up behind him. The darkness had waited until he was sated with sugar, and then the claws dug in, drawing marks in his own blood. He hadn't turned around soon enough to counter the attack. Even after Daphne died—he should have sensed it then!—he still believed in the perfect, golden light that had accompanied him through life.

This was his fault.

He'd done something wrong. Made a mess of gratitude. And now the darkness was oozing in from all corners. Leaving him with one insufficient prayer:

Don't let her heart stop beating.

After Kendra left, Lilly, more jovial than she'd been in weeks, bent over to embrace him.

"Thank you, Daddy! Thank you, thank you!"

James felt triumphant for making her so happy, but he also felt his young daughter crushing him—his face smooshed against her collarbone, her arms like a vice. If she held him much longer he'd suffocate, or the girl would break his bones. A panic started to bubble in him and he wriggled away, trying to laugh it off.

"Careful of those strong arms, Lillypod."

He took a few awkward steps away from her, masking what he truly felt. Unable to scream. Or run.

LILLY

"Please?" Lilly begged.

"Some specialists are coming, volunteers from overseas."

"I don't want to go—*please*, Daddy?"

Her dad kept his eyes on the traffic as he swerved ahead of someone. Here he was racing to get to her medical appointment on time, and it was the last place she wanted to go.

"Can't we tell them I'm—" No, they couldn't call in sick to a team of doctors. "Tell them I have something really important I need to do with my friend? Homework?"

"You can see Rain later, we'll have her over for supper."

Lilly wished she could harrumph, or kick the glove box, or tip back the bucket seat and mourn her horrible life in private. But she was too jammed in; there wasn't an inch of room to spare, even to breathe.

She couldn't make him understand the rollercoaster reality of her feelings. On the one hand the day had started great with a delivery from Kendra: a perfect, comfy pair of jeans, two cute tops (one with stars, one with butterflies), and a new book bag. She went to school feeling ordinary in a way she hadn't since the semester began. As happy as she'd been about getting fitted for a wardrobe, she hadn't taken Kendra's promises about "proportional" outfits all that seriously. But truly, her jeans and star-speckled T-shirt fit like they were *made for her.* And her backpack, draped over her shoulder, was the ideal size. Rain had oohed and aahed and wished aloud, for the millionth time, that they had their own cellphones so Lilly could snap-and-zap pictures of each garment as they arrived.

That had been the only good part of Lilly's day.

The weirdness with Declan was like a stinky fart that kept her from getting too close to people. Could they smell it on her? That she'd let a fourteen-year-old touch her boob? Was it obvious, by how she stood or looked or walked, that she'd liked it—at first? After her brain—and conscience—had clicked on she'd begun doubting everything and was now quite worried about who and what she was. A slut? Already? A slut before she'd even kissed anyone?

She really, really wanted to tell Rain *everything*, but the possible reactions made her heart jump, which in turn made her lightheaded. At best Rain might say, "*Declan*? You let Declan touch your *what*?" And even if she saw past the Brother Issue, what she'd done might sound freakish and like nothing Rain would do, at least not without consulting Lilly first.

There hadn't been time to consult Rain. Or anyone else. But it was easy to imagine Rain feeling betrayed by the who and what of it. What Lilly really wanted—needed—was for someone to tell her it was okay, that she hadn't done anything unforgiveable. But alone with only her pummeling misgivings, the more unlikely it became that she would tell anyone. Ever.

Before her gargantuan growth spurt Lilly—like Rain—had only "breast buds" (so described in a book given to them by Mrs. Shen). They were dumb, sore little nubs that had filled them with dismay. Regardless of how many colors they came in, bras looked like cranky traps meant to keep wild animals from running away. Periods were even worse. Adolescence didn't sound very promising. Pubic hair and underarm hair and darkening leg hair, as if adulthood was lurking just beneath their skin like an ogre they'd need to tend for the rest of their lives. If given the choice, she'd have preferred to skip puberty and get a cat.

But when the boobs grew in, almost overnight...Truthfully, they were better than the nubs. Rain had pushed her dresser against her bedroom door—the furniture her only lock—and Lilly lifted up her shirt. They weren't pendulous old lady boobs, or round-and-fake like a coconut bikini top. Dainty and happy-looking, Lilly's little breasts had reminded them of a painting they'd once seen in a museum, of a tree heavily laden with soft, irregular fruit. Something about the nipples had embarrassed her, the live-wire that coiled inside them, altering their shape; and then Declan had rubbed them—over shirt, over bra—and she'd finally understood. The little buggers had been reactive in a surprising and not unpleasant way.

A way she wanted again.

No. No!

So there was nothing to do but pretend with Rain that nothing had happened. Which added guilt to the guilt and Lilly worried for the first time that her body would ruin them.

Her dad zipped into the parking lot, screeching to a stop by a sign that read Patient Discharge.

Where was Rain when she needed her? Rain would take one look at that sign and snort, a preface to an eruption of laughter. Discharge. There was a paragraph about that in Mrs. Shen's Ever So Helpful book, and there it had nothing to do with dropping off frail or late humans who needed easy access to an automatic door. Their bodies were promising to ooze and stink and increase the surface space it needed to dispel their mate-attracting pheromones.

Ugh.

Lilly waited inside as her father parked in the garage. There was other stuff she couldn't tell him: she was scared—of the doctors, and what they were looking for. And the way they touched her with their cold hands. Only her original pediatrician, Dr. Benoit, still spoke to her as one would a child (a frightened child), but Dr. Benoit was no longer in charge of Her Case. Lilly was a "Case" now. A thing to be recorded. A problem to be solved. In the presence of the doctors her issue wasn't rapid growth but infectious invisibility. In their presence her true self receded, faded away, until there was just The Body. The Problem.

Per the routine, she changed into a cloth hospital gown that snapped at the neck, tied at the waist, and was covered in a design that looked like wrecked ships. It was meant for someone very, very wide not very, very tall, but it was the best they could do. For once Lilly wasn't totally mortified that the gogglers might see a flash of her underpants: Kendra made her some nice ones in soft stretchy pastel cotton that were exactly what a girl would wear, not a gramma.

She sat on the exam table, ankles crossed, hands in her lap, eyes on the wrecked ships in their pale blue sea.

Six men—seven, if she included her dad—circled her, clipboards in hand, stethoscopes around their neck. Three were doctors she saw every week and three were new, but she didn't bother to look at them or learn their names. One of them asked her dad a bunch of questions about eating and sleeping and growing while the others took turns listening to her heart and lungs.

When she grew bored of studying the gown she turned her attention to the floor. It had a splatter pattern in autumn colors that might camouflage drops of blood. She didn't want to hear what the doctors were debating. But their words snuck in.

Radiate. Pituitary. Ossification. Biopsy.

Unpleasant images turned like pages through her mind. There was the frog she'd dissected the previous year for her advanced biology class. It had been a fascinating project that made her briefly consider a career in medicine (her recent experiences quashed that). Now she possessed a more immediate understanding of being exposed and studied; of course the frog was never meant to benefit.

She also remembered standing in the archway to the Shens' living room, transfixed by what Mr. and Mrs. Shen and Declan were watching (her dad only watched sitcoms or tennis). Once there'd been a real person who was so deformed they called him the Elephant Man. Rain called for her to hurry up, but Lilly had struggled to pull herself away from the captivating imagery. Later she Googled "Elephant Man," and now she was concerned that someday someone would erect an immense glass case to display her bones.

Would she be boiled, to remove her flesh?

She sighed when one of the doctors started measuring

her. In her peripheral vision she saw he was an "old" one—she'd seen him many times—though he was the youngest of the group. He smelled of red-and-white swirls and smiled at her with peppermint eyes. He had Boy Band hair and sometimes his fingers lingered against her skin. Every week they gleefully did this, barely able to suppress their excitement at her increasing measurements. The doctors reminded her of Christopher Columbus, a man with a lofty reputation for his *discovery* of a land mass that was quite well known to the people who lived there.

"Can't we just give them Kendra's numbers?" It was the first she'd spoken and the doctors looked as if the table had come to life.

"Kendra?" One of them asked.

"She measured me yesterday, for all my new clothes."

"Let them do what they need to do, honey." Her dad said it kindly, as if he sympathized with her vulnerability, but he never said no to them. Like the doctors, he wanted the exams and data to reveal something. He wanted a cure, where she just wanted to be left alone. Lilly had started to feel like he couldn't be counted on to protect her.

It wasn't so bad when Kendra measured her. For one thing, Lilly hadn't been almost naked. For another, it resulted in the exponential increase of a desirable wardrobe. But every week the doctors measured everything: nose, ears, fingers, toes, the distance between her eyes, the diameter of her head. And when they asked her to lie back so they could check her private parts she thought she was going to die. Her legs were too long for the exam table and it was the inadequacy of *things*—furniture, cars, hand-held objects—that made her feel the most insecure. That, and the way her father turned his head. On some level she presumed he was mortified too, but he never said no.

A normal tween would wait for her father while absorbed in the complex alternate dimension of her phone. As she sat in the hallway on the double-wide chair—comforted that by its intended purpose to hold very heavy people it would not crumble beneath her—Lilly had nothing to do but eavesdrop. She couldn't assign faces to the voices in the next-door office, except for her father's. She imagined him pivoting from person to person, as the doctors were not in agreement and sometimes the voices rose to defeat a differing opinion.

"It may be experimental but we're running out—"

"The procedure's too dangerous, and right now we're seeing only millimeters of change."

"But it's just as dangerous if we wait and do nothing and things start accelerating—"

"Perhaps, but we should prioritize. Ossifications aren't the most pressing matter."

"Is she going to keep growing?" That was her dad, desperate. "If you can stop that, we can worry about the other things later."

They were quieter for a moment and Lilly pictured them nodding and mumbling.

"I think we have to consider radiation."

"Yes."

"As soon as possible."

"It's dangerous, and there isn't an obvious tumor—"

"But it's something to *try*, and it's proven successful in cases of gigantism and acromegaly."

"But we aren't even in agreement on what this is!"

"How dangerous? Dangerous how?" her father asked.

"Learning disabilities."

"Personality changes."

Lilly gripped the arm of the chair and leaned closer to the door. Being excessively tall was one thing, but at least she was still Lilly, smart and capable. She didn't want to risk losing herself.

"Oh, well that doesn't sound so bad."

Her jaw dropped at her dad's casual acceptance of the consequences.

"There isn't a guarantee—we can't be sure of either the efficacy or the side effects."

"It's our best chance to stop the process, and that remains—"

"Please fix her! Just do something!" Her father's wail silenced the room. They stopped talking so abruptly that Lilly wondered if the floor had dropped open, hungry for a snack of mean men.

"We could start next week, Monday."

"Thank you," said her dad with a gush of relief.

What were they planning on doing to her? Her Case was far outside the realms of known medicine. They were going to treat her like a humungous guinea pig.

"I'd also recommend admitting her to the hospital. Things are happening that we don't understand, she could suffer a complication at any time."

"We should definitely monitor the stress on her heart."

"Definitely."

"Now?" Her dad's voice rose with a panic that Lilly shared. "Her friend is coming for dinner and Lilly doesn't know anything about this. Could we pack a suitcase and come back tonight?"

Oh. Maybe he wasn't panicked, but…eager?

"How about we admit her on Monday. Can we all agree to that? Talk to her over the weekend. Explain that there's nothing painful about the procedure, but we want to keep an eye on her and make sure she gets the best care."

"Is it safe, will she be okay if we wait until then?" Her father sounded uneasy.

Lilly tuned them out and slumped back in the chair. She wasn't going to let them experiment on her. They didn't even know what they were doing! How could her dad agree with these horrible people?

Once upon a time she would have believed him capable of holding up the moon with one hand if it ever threatened to tumble from its place above their heads. Daddy could save her from every bad thing that lurked in the dark, and years ago she'd asked him to wrestle the big blue monster that hid beneath her bed, to scare him so he'd leave her alone. But clever Daddy had a less violent solution: a one-way ticket on the next Creature Bus—all the way to the Village of Wrong Things. The big blue monster packed up and left and never bothered her again.

But Daddy couldn't save her anymore. If he really wouldn't listen to her, take her side, she'd have to come up with a plan on her own—and might have to consider a once-unthinkable possibility: she might need to run away.

She wasn't sure how much it cost, but maybe she could catch a ride on the Creature Bus. The Village of Wrong

Things was a legend, described in a poem, but that didn't mean it wasn't real. If she could find it, maybe she could live happily ever after in a place where she wasn't so peculiar, so different, when compared to everyone else. All sorts of strange people and animals lived in the Village of Wrong Things. It made her sad to think of leaving Rain behind, but hopefully she could make new friends (even if not a best friend).

When her dad emerged from the office Lilly stood and stomped down the hall. She used the full of her stride and he ran to keep up with her.

"What's the hurry?" he called from behind.

"Something I need to do." She had to count the money in her piggy bank, which wasn't a pig but an elephant. Just in case.

JAMES

It wasn't going as he'd planned. Rain was out with her family, unavailable to be the buffer, the comfort, that Lilly needed while he told her what the doctors wanted to do. He'd counted on Rain to cheer her up. Left to do the heavy lifting himself, Lilly only stared at her plate, pushing things around with her fork.

"I'll pick Rain up every day after school and bring her to the hospital to visit." He hadn't discussed it with the Shens yet, but he felt confident they would agree. Lilly still sulked. He hated feeling like the bad guy and hadn't expected her to take it quite so badly. "She can bring your homework, so you don't fall behind. And you'll have your own room, you can watch TV together."

The brightness he added to his voice did nothing to sway his sullen daughter. He reached out, touched the back of her hand. How long had it been since he'd touched her? Did her skin feel different? Reptilian?

"Lillypod, honey? It's going to be okay. I know you're scared—"

"I don't. Want. To go. What are they even going to be doing to me?" She shot the words like arrows. His heart was the target, but she focused on his eyes. She didn't sound afraid; she sounded furious.

"They're trying to help you. They're trying..." Lilly didn't grasp what could happen if she didn't stop growing.

"Why don't I get a say in it? Why do you just let them do whatever they want?"

Where had all this rage come from? He shrank back, pulled his hand away. "I'm sorry, if it's...hard. But Lilly, this is very serious. Do you understand? There's a lot at stake if...I would die if anything happened to you."

A part of him was already dying, shriveling as Lilly grew. Once she'd had a beach ball with a tiny hole and the air slowly leaked out. How he wished he could put his finger on her defect—a stop-gap measure until a more permanent solution came along. It wouldn't be as easy as a sliver of duct tape, but they were running out of time. He also needed (though it was hard to admit) to get Lilly out of the house, and not only because he wanted someone more capable to care for her.

The sight of her was starting to sicken him. How could this abomination be made of his own genetic material? When the doctors suggested admitting her right then and there, his first instinct had been to drop to his knees and kiss their hands. If he'd kept his Best Daddy Ever mouth shut he wouldn't now have to wait out the weekend. Three nights, two days... At least they were finally going to *do* something.

Lilly's expression, her defiance, softened. A tear slid down her cheek. It melted a chamber of his treasonous heart.

"I'll stay with you in the hospital, every night." He gripped her hand. "I'm sorry it has to be like this."

"Me too," she whispered, defeated. "May I be excused?"

"You aren't hungry?" She shook her head. "Okay. There are leftovers, if you change your mind."

With her chin already on her chest, she didn't have as far to duck as she left the kitchen. When he heard her bedroom door shut, James brought his hands to his face and wept. Would either of them survive this metamorphosis?

Kendra arrived early as promised, before Lilly was even awake, so James could give her a happy surprise (and alleviate a tad of his guilt). The seamstress and her elves had been busy—they'd made another pair of jeans, a denim skirt, the promised hoodie, multiple shirts. Even a pair of pajamas. Lilly's taste formerly had a bit of flash and flare, and rarely included ruffles or soft colors. Perhaps it was her recent dependence on men's clothing, and his or Kendra's influence, but her new wardrobe struck him as more feminine.

As he draped her new clothes over the living room furniture, he remembered the Christmases from when she was very young. His mother remained his inspiration, a magician when it came to holidays and celebrations. She thrived on decorating, baking, expressing her love through the thematic opportunities bestowed on them by special days. He and Lilly celebrated Christmas as he had as a child, and all of the grandparents participated. She'd go to bed in her ordinary house, and awaken to a wonderland filled with sweets and wrapped gifts, a magical tree, and the twinkling smiles of her beloved family.

A living room full of clothing wasn't exactly the same, but he hoped it would trigger fond memories. He wanted to remind her how much she was loved; it was the least he could do. No. Sadly it was the most he could do, as he was otherwise bereft.

When Lilly finally emerged from her room, barefoot in the blue jeans she'd received the day before (and the butterfly shirt she hadn't yet worn), James stood and tried to keep the smile from avalanching off his face. The first thing he noticed—something he most definitely didn't want to see—was a slip of ankle, visible below the hem of her pants. They had fit differently the day before.

Lilly had grown during the night.

"Surprise!" he said, hoping she interpreted his emotion as tears of joy, not sorrow. Not alarm or despair.

Her face brightened as she took in the array of clothes, her eyes traveling from item to item. She fingered the material of the soft pajamas.

"Everything's so nice," she said, almost a whisper.

"Want to try it all on? Have a little fashion show?"

It's what he'd always intended, but now he also wanted to make sure the garments still fit. There was no point in Kendra racing to finish more if Lilly already needed bigger sizes.

Lilly nodded, eager, and scooped up the clothing.

"Before you—" James glanced at his watch. "Want to wait just a minute? Rain will be here soon."

When Rain hadn't been available the previous evening, James made arrangements for her to come as the "VIP audience" for Lilly's fashion show. Zhao, Rain's dad, would be dropping her off momentarily.

James expected Lilly to give her signature bounce (if her knees still worked well enough) upon hearing of her best friend's imminent arrival, but instead a cloud passed over her face, dampening her joy.

"Rain's coming?"

He couldn't understand why this was anything but good news. "Yes? Is that...?"

"That's fine." Arms full of clothes, she headed for her room. "Just call me when she's here."

"She's so excited to see what you got."

"I know." Once again, she sealed herself inside her room.

James didn't understand what was happening. His daughter was growing distant, moody, challenging in ways he hadn't expected. He couldn't imagine Rain being cross to Lilly, or saying anything that would damage their friendship—and all of the Shens were concerned about her health. James kept Michelle, Rain's mom, up to date on Lilly's situation.

Before he could ponder it further he heard a car door slam; he was there to greet Rain before she even knocked. He waved goodbye to Zhao, who *toot-tooted* the horn in farewell. Across the street James spotted a white van covered with stickers, its skulking occupant pointing a long-lensed camera toward his house. Bloody press. James gave him the finger and turned away.

Rain bounded in, bringing with her the scent of watermelon shampoo and a youthful vitality that he realized, suddenly, was missing from his house. As Lilly grew, the playful and innocent and optimistic elements of their existence, once taken for granted, were sucked out of the air as if they fed some vampiric creature. Now that he recognized it, he could almost see the shadowy ghost hovering near the ceiling, waiting to drift down and poison them when they ran out of reasons to be hopeful. Rain, in spite of her name, was nothing short of sunshine and James hoped she would do more than brighten Lilly's day. Was it too much to ask of a tween to replenish their atmosphere?

"Hi!" she said with a grin.

"So happy you're...Lilly, Rain's here!"

"Lilly, come strut your stuff!" She plopped onto the sofa, ready to be entertained.

"Out in a sec!"

Nothing in Rain's behavior indicated she had any reservations about seeing Lilly, so whatever was happening was on Lilly's end. Perhaps his daughter's anxiety was worse than he knew, and starting to manifest in anger and frustration. Or maybe...Was Lilly aware that she could die?

Terminally ill people sometimes pushed away their loved ones, thinking that if they don't feel as close to the dying person, their death will hurt them less. Oh no...This was a whole new level of nightmarish if Lilly *felt* like she was dying. As soon as the fashion show was over James would sneak off to his office and call the doctors. (If she was smaller he might have hoisted her up and rushed to the hospital that minute.) For now, he couldn't let himself panic and risk ruining his daughter's happy morning. He focused on Rain—sunshine—and the effortless way she radiated glee and anticipation.

"Have you eaten?" he asked her. "Lilly hasn't had breakfast yet, so I'll be making some eggs and toast. Want anything to drink?"

"I might have a nibble, but I'm good. I just wanna see Lilly. Lilly, come on!"

And there she was. Lilly's door opened and she pranced out, quite gracefully (even with her thick, cumbersome feet), wearing the floral-patterned blouse tucked into the denim skirt. Her reservations about Rain's arrival seemed to have been forgotten. She strutted past the furniture and stood near the kitchen entryway, from which she could give them an unobstructed view of her modeling. Hand on her waist, she turned one way, then another, showing them her outfit from multiple angles.

Grinning ecstatically, Rain squealed and clapped her hands. "Holy galoshes, Lilly! You look so grown up!"

James had noticed the same thing, but it wasn't something that made him cheer. The shirt's pattern looked too mature for her, and it fit... It didn't hide her breasts the way the overly large menswear had, or even the way her new boxy T-shirts did. It aged her in a way he didn't like, making her look womanly.

"It fits *perfectly*!" said Rain.

"This is my favorite." She did a little spin, although the skirt's heavy denim didn't flair. "Kendra is a *genius*!"

James was pretty sure Kendra had measured the skirt to come to Lilly's knees, and now it stopped just above them. Lilly seemed unaware of the height she'd gained during the night. Perhaps from her perspective it was so incremental as to not matter.

"Do you like it, Daddy?"

"You look beautiful, honey." And she did. His angel. His sweet little angel who wasn't going to survive. He ducked into the kitchen for a cup of coffee so the girls wouldn't see him cry.

illy tried on different combinations of all her new garments. Her other favorites were the boot cut jeans—which looked naturally faded as if she'd worn them for years (and had length to spare)—and the red hoodie with the kangaroo pocket. This outfit, too, filled James with emotion. It was just the sort of thing little Lilly would have worn, with her glittery silver high-tops.

"That is *so* you!" Rain gushed.

So Lilly. Who she had been. And now, exponentially larger in every direction, this version of her was like a sponge that soaked up too much water. This was Lilly, exaggerated. Stretched on a rack. A little girl plumped with treats before the witch devoured her. The resemblance to her former self was more than James could take. Ever since the previous day's appointment his waking moments were accompanied by a clock that ticked louder and faster with each advancing hour. He wracked his brain, certain that in his youth he'd read a story of a boy who grew too fast, and to cure him the father...

Procured some special fruit from a strange land?

Made selfless promises to a troll?

Hadn't there been a tale of a beautiful woman who, every midnight, turned into a witch? And a man loved her without showing preference for her silky self or her warty one, for which she rewarded him by returning his afflicted little boy to good health. But where to find such a woman? He'd only dated sporadically since Daphne's death, and none of the online dating sites offered such a match.

Every day their predicament found a new way to torture him and James was struggling to maintain the usual routines of their lives.

"Gonna scramble some eggs," he said, retreating to the kitchen. As he whisked, then spooned the congealing yellow around in the pan, he heard Lilly and Rain from the other room. Lilly's voice hadn't changed. From afar, they were two ordinary eleven-year-old girls, a few weeks into middle school, giggling over familiar things. Along with the dozen eggs, he toasted ten slices of bread.

He carried his plate, with its meager portion, through the living room. "Breakfast's all ready—I'll leave you girls to it. You know where to find me."

"Thanks, Daddy!"

He hoped his retreat was seen as a gesture of kindness, of consideration that his growing daughter (even if she hadn't physically grown so much) needed more privacy with her friends. When he was sure she couldn't see him, he ran to his office and shut the door. He needed the specialists. He needed the rabbit hole of the internet with its conspiracy theories and professional quacks. He needed to call his parents. Someone out there had to tell him there was a cure, that everything would be fine, or he wasn't sure he could go on being a person, a functioning human, never mind the dad his daughter needed.

Once he'd had a weird reaction to a medication that left him feeling like his veins were on fire, like his muscles were controlled by a switchboard helmed by drunk kittens. But what had bothered him most was the effect it had on his brain—on his thoughts and inability to communicate. Every word traveled in its own helium balloon, neatly labeled.

He saw the thoughts he wanted, the things he wanted to say, as they drifted away. His non-functioning hand hadn't been able to reach up and grab the words, so there'd been no way to explain to onlookers how desperately wrong he felt.

It was like that now. A panic that wouldn't conform to words. A tragedy that, like the elevated pitch of a moron sucking in helium, looked humorous at first. Lilly the Friendly Giant. But irreplaceable brain cells were killed by that idiotic balloon. Lilly's affliction was a reality he had to accept, but struggled to believe. Given the fantastical and deadly nonsense of his life, who should he summon for a cure? A clown?

He clamped a hand over his mouth so the girls couldn't hear the bubbles of tainted laughter that escaped from his throat. In the tri-reflections of his screens he weighed which clown to summon first.

LILLY

illy let Rain do the gabbing while she, ravenous from having skipped dinner, snarfed up her eggs. Rain nibbled on a piece of toast and told a story about Declan from the previous night, how he'd intentionally messed up his spoken Chinese so he made nonsensical sentences that horrified their grandparents.

"They thought he had a brain tumor!" Rain said, laughing. "Or that he was on drugs. And they blamed it on my *dad*!"

Lilly couldn't help but laugh, but the mention of Declan ignited a briquette of remorse in her gut.

"And then my parents were like, begging him to 'act normal.' Like he's even capable of that. And then once my grandparents understood he was just joking around they got mad at my dad *again*, because he'd raised such a disrespectful son. And then Declan did what he always does, gets all charming, speaks perfect Chinese, apologizes to everyone. That's how he gets whatever he wants, it's so unfair."

Whatever he wants. Was Lilly something he'd wanted? The thought of it made the eggs in her tummy start to thrum, in a bad, gonna-throw-up kind of way.

"You okay? You look a little...?"

Lilly put her fork down and pushed her plate away. She wanted to tell Rain everything—about *everything!*— but wasn't sure where to start. Abandoning her breakfast, she quickly rose (bonking her head on the light fixture) and grabbed Rain's hand. "Let's go talk in my room, it's more private."

After Rain skipped in behind her, Lilly shut the door. Her dad had moved her mattress onto the floor the previous day, before taking the bedframe to the cobwebby cellar. She'd been mad at first, even though he'd explained it would be more comfortable to sleep nearer the ground, where her feet would be supported. And she wouldn't be in danger of the frame collapsing if she flopped over too heavily in the middle of the night. Her dad had been right. With her arms and legs stretched out on the fuzzy carpet she'd felt so much less confined, and finally got a decent night's sleep.

Rain sat on a corner of the mattress, diagonally from Lilly, whose legs took up the rest of the space. In sputtering bursts, she told Rain what had happened with Declan in the basement, spurred on by the fear that her friend would run home mad before Lilly could finish. And Rain was mad. But not in the way Lilly anticipated.

"What an asshole! I'm gonna kill him!"

"It wasn't totally his fault," said Lilly, still haunted by the guilt of it.

"Do you know how often my mom has talked to us about *boundaries*? About *consent*? Declan totally crossed the line—my parents are gonna kill him too!"

"Please don't tell them!" Lilly begged.

"Why? The little turd deserves to be punished, he gets away with everything."

"Because then my father will know. He has this whole idea of me as his 'little girl.' And he's already so messed up about my *size*." Lilly shook her head, imagining her father's disappointment. "He couldn't handle it, Rain. He doesn't want to think about, you know, that part of me that's growing up normally. And, I know it's your brother, but imagine it was…some other boy. And it felt…not that bad."

"I get it." Rain wilted a little, disappointed that she couldn't get Declan in heaps of trouble. "I guess, if I'd been in your shoes…I would've done the same thing."

"You think?" Hope fluttered inside her.

"Yeah. Probably. Don't feel bad, Lilly. But…Be careful. Even Declan, who knows better, is a complete asshat. Other boys might be worse."

Rain's advice was an echo of her brother's.

"I don't think it'll happen again," Lilly said, brimming with more confidence. "It was a little too confusing, and I think I'm too…maybe when I'm thirteen."

"Yeah. In a couple years."

"Yeah."

"And you should know—my mom would tell you this— you can be *mean* if you have to. If they don't understand what no means, or if they won't stop. Gouge their eyes out, or knee them in the balls." Lilly giggled. "I'm serious. And you've got size on your side."

Lilly buried her face in her pillow, laughing at the image of herself trampling some frisky boy. She should've told Rain sooner; Rain understood *everything* like no one else.

"You're the best."

"I know. So what did the doctors say?" her friend asked. "I know your dad called my mom."

Lilly smooshed the pillow over her face again, groaning this time. Rain tugged at her pants leg.

"Tell me. You'll scare me even more if you don't tell me."

Her head thumped against the wall as Lilly leaned back, tossing the pillow aside. "It's so messed up. The doctors have this idea, an experiment they want to try to see if they can get me to stop growing. I think they want to destroy something in my brain."

Rain's face contorted, aghast with fear and disgust. "You serious?"

"I mean, I might just stop growing on my own. And the 'procedure' as they like to call it could have these horrible side effects."

"Like what?"

"Like learning disabilities, or my personality might totally change."

"No way! Your dad would never go along with—"

"He scheduled it for *Monday*!"

Rain sat there, mouth agape, in utter shock. And then to Lilly's horror, Rain's eyes welled with tears.

"Don't...Rain!" She scooted across the mattress and took her friend's tiny hand in hers.

"I don't want you to become someone else! I'm already so afraid—" Rain stopped herself.

"Afraid of what?"

Rain chewed on her lip for a minute, gazing at Lilly with a tormented expression. "Afraid of...What if something happens? And we can't be friends anymore."

"That won't ever happen. You'll *always* be my best friend."

"The doctors will change you even more."

"No, no—I won't let them. I have a plan."

Rain looked a smidge more hopeful. She wiped at her eyes, her attention fixed on Lilly. "How are you gonna get out of it? Will your dad come around?"

Lilly shook her head. "He won't listen. But I'm going to run away."

"Really? Where?" Suddenly she radiated excitement.

"I think there might be a place where...not monsters, I don't believe in monsters anymore. But a place for people who are different. I'm going to see if I can find it."

For a moment Rain just blinked. Lilly crossed-her-fingers that her friend wouldn't notice the downside of her plan—that she didn't know exactly, positively where she was going. While Lilly no longer believed that the beasts from her nightmares could materialize beneath her bed (especially in its current condition), she'd had to rethink some things since becoming a giant. If she was possible, then other oddities were too. She was living proof, and maybe there were other giants who'd hidden themselves away, afraid of medical experiments that would change their personalities. It seemed possible now that fairytales could be based on a reality that most people didn't personally experience.

Before Rain could object or try to talk her out of it, Lilly tried to explain. "Remember that poem I always loved? *The Village of Wrong Things*? The bigger I get, the more likely it seems that other...things, animals, people...There could be other people like me, and the world just wants to study them, or make fun of them, so they've found their own place to live. The poem is a clue, for people who need it. And this—" she gestured toward her window. "—is just a small town, what do we know about what's out there? I know my dad wants a quick solution. He wants me back as I was and that isn't going to happen. No one's giving me the option to just...be who I am. This doesn't have to be a bad thing. Maybe I...belong somewhere else."

"I'm coming with you." It was so decisive. Rain gripped her hand, hard.

"Really?" She hadn't considered that Rain might want to come, and it filled her with joy.

"You need me. If you belong somewhere else, then I do too. Buddy system. And I'll make sure you don't get in over your head—haha!"

"We have to leave tomorrow," Lilly whispered, excited to have a partner-in-crime.

"We'll need some money."

"I already thought of that. I have seventy dollars."

"I have a bank account, for my birthday money n' stuff. I'll go to the supermarket with my dad later—get to an ATM."

"Thank you!" She grabbed her friend into a gentle bear hug. "Should I try to steal some more? From my dad?" The words came out softer than a whisper.

"Maybe. We might be on the road for a while. Do you know which direction—"

A knock came loud as a crack of lightning on her door. Both girls jumped, their faces mirrored masks of surprise. Lilly didn't know how her dad could have overheard them, but worried he had. When he opened the door and stuck his head in, she recognized the fake smile. The nervous wandering of his eyes. He had more bad news to deliver, and was trying to hide it.

"Hey girls, can I come in a sec?"

Lilly nodded. Rain moved to squeeze in beside her so they both reclined against the wall, ready for a lecture.

"So, I just got off the phone with..." He rubbed his hands together, glanced around the room. "I'm glad you're here Rain, you can...You're such a great friend."

The girls looked at each other. They *both* knew bad news was coming.

"I know we weren't going to go into the hospital until Monday, but I'm worried..." The forged smile fell off. In its place was anguish—enough anguish that to see it on her father's face punctured a hole in Lilly's heart. In response, she gripped Rain's hand so hard she cried out.

"Ow!"

"Sorry."

"I've arranged...I think it's better if we head in tomorrow, right after I get back from church—maybe you'll want to go with me? The hospital is expecting us, and they'll get a room ready just for you, with everything you'll need. A big TV, and a big comfy bed—and an extra bed so you can have sleepovers, just like we talked about." He tried to get the smile to settle again, but it wobbled like it wasn't quite attached to his skin.

"Okay." That's all Lilly said.

Her dad nodded and slunk away.

Rain turned to Lilly and panic-whispered, "You aren't really going are you?"

The most devious smile of Lilly's eleven years bloomed on her face.

LILLY

Lilly did as she was told and filled her new backpack with all her new clothes. When Daddy told her not to forget her toothbrush she chewed on her grin so it wouldn't show. These were all the things she needed anyway, even if she had no intention of taking them to the hospital.

Her dad had recently started going to church, something they rarely did before unless her grandparents invited them. Lilly went with him only once: the little kids kneeled on their wooden pews and stared at her; most of the adults had stared too.

Now, when she wasn't having a Saturday night sleepover at Rain's, her dad sometimes let her stay home alone on Sunday mornings—with strict admonishments to keep the doors locked and not answer the phone unless she recognized the caller. It was the perfect set up to execute her plan and it didn't matter at all that Daddy had changed his mind about when to take her to the hospital. By sticking to his Sunday routine he was giving her the perfect window of opportunity.

Rain would meet her at the school playground at 10:05am—it was the one place they were allowed to walk to by themselves, conveniently situated just a couple of blocks between their two houses. Their parents believed they were then heading to the other's house: Lilly to Rain's; Rain to Lilly's. It would buy them some time to get to the bus station and slip away.

As her dad fixed a blue striped noose around his neck, Lilly stretched out on the sofa and flipped on the TV. *Look casual.* She wore her denim skirt and flowery blouse—the outfit that made her appear most mature—hoping she could be mistaken for a young woman, able to travel on her own.

"You're packed for when I get back?" The car keys dangled from his finger.

"Yup."

"Okay, well, I won't be long. Call my cell if you need anything. Don't answer—"

"I know," she tried to sound more annoyed than she actually felt. The truth was, in spite of her desperation to stop the doctors from tinkering with the delicate structures in her skull, she wished she didn't have to leave home. In the urgency of planning and plotting with Rain there'd only been excitement. But now the reality hit her. She wouldn't get to go to school anymore, or sleep in her room. Or live with her dad.

If she found what she was looking for—and proved to him that she could live a long life as a giant—maybe he would join her in the Village of Wrong Things. Then he could make the doctors understand that there was nothing wrong with being tall, or oversize, or different, and she and Rain could come back home. Lilly would happily advocate for all the other oddballs who'd hidden themselves away, and maybe they'd be able to come home, too.

It was too late to wish that things had gone differently, but leaving filled her with sadness. What if this was the last time she ever saw her dad? To keep from crying, she kept her eyes on the television and pretended she didn't care. About him leaving. About the hospital. About anything.

"Bye," she said as he headed for the door.

"Bye, Lillypod." He lingered with his hand on the knob.

Was he having second thoughts? Lilly almost hoped so. If he didn't leave, her plan would be ruined, but maybe... Maybe she could plead her case to the doctors and find some sort of compromise.

Her dad opened the door—"Mr. Wolf!"—and immediately shut it.

"What's going on? Crows?" Lilly sat up, startled. Had a flock gathered on the roof? That happened sometimes, when the crows got aggressive and started barking every name they knew.

"Afraid not. It's the local news channel." He sidestepped to the front window and peered out. "They've left several messages."

"They have?"

"Want an interview. I keep saying no." He closed the living room curtains and the darkness made Lilly's courage deflate even more. It was daunting to imagine having to do everything by herself, become an adult sooner than she was ready. She got up and wandered over to the window, took a tiny peek.

"Do you want me to stay?" her dad asked.

The question surprised her. A part of her desperately wanted to say yes. *Stay. Don't leave me.* But the TV crew on her doorstep made her predicament even more real. She didn't want the whole world following her story, making comments and judgements, or offering their thoughts and prayers as they dismantled her brain, dissected her personality. She just wanted to be a tall girl who did all the things a short girl did.

There was no answer for "What's it like to be so tall?" What was it like to have eyelashes? Or elbows, or freckles? Everyone only asked her stupid questions. If only someone had bothered to ask "Do I have dandruff in my hair?" or "Can you change the lightbulb in the ceiling?" Then she would've felt useful, appreciated. Behind the questions was an unspoken assumption: Do you hate it? Are you miserable? And she wasn't. Sure, she was scared sometimes; everything was changing and no one seemed happy about it. Why couldn't anyone gaze at her and say, "Gosh, aren't you the most amazing girl ever!"? (Would a mommy have done that?)

There was nothing left for her here, in the place she knew as home.

"No, it's okay," she said. "I'll keep the doors locked."

"I'll be back in an hour. If they get too close or start knocking on the door or bothering you, call me, okay? They're not allowed to trespass." He stopped at the door again. "You sure, Lillypod?"

She could tell he really wanted to go, while also wanting to stay. That time at church he'd intertwined his hands in prayer so tightly his fingernails turned purple. He needed to pray now. He needed to pray the way she needed to run away. But just in case it was their last chance, she bent down to give him a hug.

Her father stepped back to avoid her reaching arms. He

blew her a kiss. "Be back soon. Love you."

"Love you too." It sounded as weak as his; Daddy didn't like her to touch him anymore. For the first time Lilly felt truly ugly.

"Mr. Wolf!" the voice came again as he reopened the door.

"Please step away—I've got nothing to say and Lilly isn't here, you're wasting your time."

"Please step away—" said a bird (probably a robin, judging by the sweetness of its voice). Robins were her favorites; they could be quite conversational, even when their responses didn't make sense. At least they tried.

She heard the click as her dad's key turned the deadbolt. Ducking down, she inched the curtain back to monitor what was happening. Her dad spat "No comment" to every inquiry until he slammed the car door, sealing himself inside. As he pulled out of the driveway the robins murmured prettily "No comment, no comment," and the TV crew retreated to the sidewalk.

The time had come to execute the final preparations before she had to leave. If she was lucky, the news people would take her dad at his word and abandon their post. But if not, she'd use her long legs and stride right past them. First, she turned off the television (her only easy task).

She felt terrible doing the next part, like the worst daughter ever, but Lilly went into her father's office, opened the middle drawer of his desk, and found the zippered pouch where he kept a supply of cash. He'd never kept it a secret from her, and she'd never considered stealing from him before. But now she needed to buy bus tickets, and food, and she had no idea how long she and Rain might be on the road. Her dad had $380. Lilly took $300.

On second thought, she took it all.

After checking the kitchen clock, she made a few peanut butter sandwiches using all of the remaining bread. Her dad bought six loaves at a time, but they were running low on...everything. Daddy would miss her, and worry about her, but on some level her leaving might be a relief. His stress hung between them like something heavy he couldn't push aside. It was going to smother him, all that worrying about her body, and how much money it was costing. The custom-made clothing, the endless trips to the supermarket, the weekly visits to the doctor (most of the researchers were volunteers, eager to study her, but Lilly knew health insurance and copays were expensive). She drooped at the thought of being such a burden.

The last thing she did was set the note on the kitchen table, between the salt and pepper shakers. She'd written it the night before, to let her dad know why she'd left. Hopefully it would keep him from worrying too much. She slipped on her backpack, looked around the only home she'd ever known, and opened the front door.

"Lilly!"
"Lilly!"
"Lilly!"

In the moment it took to understand what was going

on—that the birds were gone and the press had multiplied since her dad's departure—the reporters and camera-people surged toward where she stood paralyzed on the little stoop.

"Are you still growing, Lilly?"

"Are you the tallest girl who's ever lived?"

"What does it feel like to be a giant?"

They snapped photos and thrust microphones in the general upward direction of her face. The video cameras took her in from toe to head, head to toe, and it reminded her of the machines at the hospital, invading her skin, revealing all the parts of her that she'd expected to remain hidden.

A swarm of stinging yellow jackets buzzed inside her, urging her to move. Going back inside wasn't an option: Rain was expecting her. Lilly's instinct told her to *run*.

The tiny adults scampered out of her way as she galloped past them. But to her horror, some of them gave chase and ran behind her. As she raced down the sidewalk, a couple of the news vans kept pace beside her in the street.

"Lilly! We just want to talk for a minute!"

Above the din of people came one frantic woman. "Don't chase her! She's a child! Lilly, come back!"

Even with her long stride she couldn't outrun the vans. She darted left and cut across a yard, but when she emerged onto the street behind the house a van screeched around the corner, almost catching up with her.

Yelling. She heard yelling. A drumbeat and a guitar riff of voices. A heavy metal pounding with squealing solos. She lost track of what they were asking, though some of the lyrics sounded desperate, urging her to be careful, slow down.

She cut across yards, made quick turns, hid behind fences when the hunters got too close. The running hurt. Her legs. Her lungs. They burned and she imagined them as two marshmallows over a campfire, engulfed in flames. She breathed the black sugar singe, the crumbling carbon, but it couldn't sustain her.

Finally she stopped, hands on her lumpy knees, her throat sore from heaving in the useless air. Her heart felt as large and heavy as a watermelon. The wrongness of it scared her: this wasn't how her body should feel or react. Her beating heart threatened to push all her other organs out of the way, and when she vomited she half-expected to find her liver on the sidewalk at her feet.

At least she'd outrun the reporters.

That helped her calm down, and her innards shrank back to their proper size—still large, but not all a jumble like a poorly packed suitcase.

It was a short-lived victory. Taking in the world around her—the shops and busy street and zooming cars—made her heart throb again. Nothing looked familiar. She'd run blindly, making turn after turn. She was nowhere near the school, or near Rain's house.

Lilly stood there with her searching eyes and disbelief. But it was true.

She was lost.

JAMES

Church helped. It was a quiet hour in a world of increasing noise. The minister gave him a kind smile, and included Lilly on the prayer list. Yet, James was glad when the service was over and he hurried to get home. The bomb was still ticking; he heard it everywhere he went. When he pulled into the driveway there was no sign of the TV van that had been there when he left. But as soon as he got out of the car a young woman with a camera around her neck raced up to him.

"Mr. Wolf!"

"I have nothing to say—"

"It's about Lilly—"

He kept his back to her as he stood on the stoop and unlocked...The deadbolt didn't click. He was sure he'd locked it when he left.

"Mr. Wolf I'm so sorry! They scared Lilly away."

It was as if he'd arrived at the wrong house, in the wrong year, on the wrong planet. For a moment he wasn't sure if he should push on inside, where Lilly would be watching TV, or give this too-young-to-be-a-real-reporter a moment to explain. She barreled on before he could choose.

"Lilly came out—no one thought she'd just take off running! I tried to get them to stop, she's just a child. The crews didn't come back, but neither did Lilly. I waited. To tell you. I'm sure they didn't mean for this to happen."

The words clucked and clattered in his head and James didn't have time to sort it out in the presence of—was her hair naturally navy-blue? He passed through the safe gateway of his home, so determined to see his child—some version of her, small or tall—lazing on the sofa with a bowl of cereal that for a moment he actually saw her, and breathed a sigh of relief.

"Lilly. Thank God." The navy-haired reporter had just been another kook. But then his daughter dissolved and there was nothing but the darkened house. "Lilly?"

He checked her room, his room, the bathroom, the office. When he got to the kitchen he couldn't miss the note; it flashed like the hazard lights on his car and he knew he didn't want to read it. But it signaled its urgency and, unsure what else to do, he plucked it out from between the salt and pepper shakers.

Dear Daddy,

I know everything that's going on has been very hard for you. I'm sorry. I know you think the doctors can help me, but I really really really think they have no idea what they're doing. I don't want people messing around in my head. Plus, I think I have a better solution. Remember that poem from the book with the fables and nursery rhymes? I'm going to look for The Village of Wrong Things! Don't freak out—I know what you're thinking! I think it IS real! I am PROOF that weird things happen! Rain is coming with me, *so you don't have to worry that I'm alone. Sorry about taking your money.* ☹ *I will send you postcards from my travels. And when I find the village maybe you can come see me??? I'll miss you Daddy. So much.*

    Love,

    Your daughter, Lilly

James spun one way, then the other, unsure what to do first. Call Rain's parents? Call the police? Go look for her? His heart hammered *your fault, your fault* but he didn't have time to wallow in guilt. He raced for the front door, where the photographer was still standing.

"Where did she go? What time?"

The young woman pointed toward the school. "About an hour—"

"I need you to help me!"

She nodded, ready for his instructions. "I'm so sorry—"

"I'm calling the police." He marched toward his car and she followed. "And I'll drive around looking for her. Can you get this on the news? Tell them Lilly is missing?"

"Yes! Absolutely! I'm sorry, I thought she'd circle back when things calmed down. Maybe she still will."

But James knew it wasn't the reporters who had scared her off. Lilly ran away. And it was his fault. He knew it to the core of his fatherly soul: he bollixed it. He'd been avoiding her, because it was too painful to look at her. And she read his downcast eyes as rejection. As he backed out of the driveway the photographer was already on the phone, but he had one more instruction for her.

"Tell them she's sick! Terribly sick. She needs to get to the hospital the minute she's found."

The color drained from the young woman's face. "I'll tell them."

The back bumper scraped against the concrete as he accelerated into the street. He sped toward the school, slowing down only to see if Lilly and Rain were chatting on the swings—in case they'd changed their minds.

As he scanned the area he dialed nine-one-one. "I need to report a missing girl."

They asked him questions. He told them about the note, the time she left, her age, and what she looked like. He told them she might be with another girl and neither of them had a cellphone. Never had he been more furious with himself. All the reasons he'd given for denying her a phone, and never had he contemplated its potential role in saving her life. It had been inconceivable that they'd ever need GPS to track her down. But here they were.

Suddenly he doubted everything he'd ever done as a parent, every rule he'd ever made, every fantasy he'd found comfort in. As if their magical dome, inflated with fatherly patience (not unlike her beach ball), would ever have been elastic enough to survive Lilly's inevitable growth. His pathetic imagination had refused the possibility that Lilly would someday possess the ability—or will—to walk out the front door.

The police asked him to return home where they could talk with him further, and in case Lilly came back. But James knew his daughter wasn't going to change her mind. She was on a mission, a foolhardy fantasy to find a place that existed only within the pages of a children's book. James ever-so-didn't want to go back to his empty house. He drove a little faster toward the main thoroughfare, heading for the bus station—Lilly's likeliest escape route. Before disconnecting with the authorities he promised to come home soon, but first he needed to see if Lilly was downtown.

He scanned the pedestrians as he drove—hoping to see his daughter's towering head—and called the Shens.

"Hey James," Michelle said as she answered the phone.

"Are the girls there?"

"Rain's here."

"Is Lilly with her?"

"No, they were supposed to meet at the playground but Lilly didn't show. What's going on?"

"She ran away!" His voice rose in hysteria now that he was talking to a fellow parent, a friend. "They were supposed to go together!"

"What? Rain, come here!"

As he neared the bus station he slowed, peering into the huge windows to see if Lilly was in the waiting area. Over his phone he heard a heated discussion between Michelle and Rain. Sure enough, Rain knew about the plan, and had meant to accompany Lilly.

Now James realized that the press, indeed, were partly to blame. Lilly hadn't made her rendezvous because the TV crews had chased her, and she'd either intentionally avoided leading them to her friend, or...Or she'd gotten turned around and hadn't been able to find her way back.

"I'll call you later!" As he hung up he heard Michelle yelling his name, but he didn't have time. He double-parked in front of the bus station, hazard-lights blinking the words from his daughter's letter—*sorry, proof, love*—and raced inside to look for her.

As terrible as it was that she'd run away, it was a thousand times worse that Rain wasn't with her.

His little Lilly was all alone.

LILLY

Lilly took a moment to survey the traffic before deciding which way to head. She was pretty sure—well, kind of sure—that a right turn would take her to the medical complex (the absolute last place she wanted to go), but from there she knew how to get downtown. If only she had a cellphone and could let Rain know where she was. Maybe Rain would find her way to the bus station, though Lilly had to consider the possibility that she was on her own.

Concerned that her conspicuous height was like a giant neon nametag with flashing arrows—Here's Lilly!—she slipped into her red hoodie and flung the hood over her head. At least her hair was no longer visible, nor her face in profile. The sleeves were a fraction shorter than they had been, and while Lilly knew what that meant, she didn't care.

They'd learned in school, from a police officer, that people who walked assertively were less likely to become victims of a crime. So Lilly walked assertively. Cars sped by and she pretended she'd done this a million times and knew exactly where she was going.

"Lilly!"

Fudge. She couldn't see who was calling her name,

but she guessed a TV van had caught up with her. Though tempted to run, she didn't want to get lost again and when she glanced ahead she recognized where she was: the dreaded medical center was just a few blocks farther. She walked a little faster.

In her peripheral vision a vehicle made a quick U-turn and slowed down beside her.

"Lilly!"

"Leave me alone."

"Lilly it's me!"

Someone she knew? It didn't sound like someone she knew. But just in case, she peeked around her hood to get a better look at the white van that was cruising alongside her. There were stickers on the windows and doors. Lightning bolts and skulls and zombies with guitars—and no TV logos; she would've remembered if she'd seen it before.

"Can I give you a ride somewhere? You going home?" The van pulled into the parking lane and Lilly finally stopped to look at the driver through the open passenger window.

A young man. With a goofy grin. He used his tongue to twirl a peppermint candy to the other side of his mouth, and that's when Lilly placed him: the young doctor with the perfect Boy Band hair—though the sunlight brought out the lines around his eyes, making him appear older. Maybe he was closer to her dad's age than she'd realized. His presence soured her mood and she marched on.

"I'm not going to the hospital," she said angrily.

He lurched along in his stickered van. "I'm not going there either. I'm done for the day, I was heading home. What's the problem? What's going on?"

When she stopped, he braked. She stooped down and considered him. He was part of the enemy team that wanted to turn her into a brainless zombie like the stupid stickers on his stupid van. But dressed in jeans and a T-shirt, tattoos on both arms, he looked less like a doctor and more like the lead singer of a band.

"I'm leaving town," she said. It wasn't a secret. "You're not gonna fudge up my brain."

He nodded, weighing her words. "I don't blame you."

"Really?" His sympathy surprised her.

"Look, I'm a researcher—I specialize in triggers for excessive growth—but I don't usually work with real people."

"What do you work with?" Unreal people?

"Mice, usually."

Something about that made her laugh. Until she imagined him sticking needles into squirming innocent mice.

"Well I'm not an experiment. I'm a real person. There's somewhere I need to go, where I'll be accepted just as I am." She resumed walking. He resumed inching beside her, though sometimes he had to swerve into traffic to get around a parked car.

"That's cool, I get it—I think I'd feel the same way. So... Am I to infer that you're running away?"

She held her head high. "Yup."

"Okay, so can I point out a flaw in your plan? I take it you're heading for the bus station?"

She stopped again. He stopped too. What was he getting at? What was wrong with her plan? She bent down and peered into the van.

"They'll look there first," he said. "It's the natural place to start. We don't have a train station, and if you wanted to fly somewhere a person without a car would probably go to the bus station to get out to the airport. If you don't want to be found, you need to lay low—not do exactly what they expect."

Hmm. He had a valid point. She surveyed the street—ahead of her, behind her. Where could she go? Could she hide in Rain's basement for a while? Or would Declan rat her out?

"Lilly, I'd do the same thing if I were you. I wouldn't want them—or me—mucking about in my head. They're guessing, because they don't know what else to do. But you're right to be skeptical. Let me help you. You can sit in the back—" He gestured behind him. There weren't any seats, but the floor was carpeted.

"Is that a beanbag?" she asked, spotting the misshapen lump behind the driver's seat.

"I'll take you to my place. You can lay low. And then—and I'm not saying you have to—if you change your mind you can call your dad. Or if not...Tomorrow I can drive you to the bus station the next town over. They won't be looking for you there." He flicked a switch and the side door started sliding open.

Lilly wasn't supposed to get into a stranger's car. But she wasn't sure if he counted, seeing how she had weekly appointments where he measured every inch of her body. Her dad trusted him (though he wasn't acting like a medical professional at the moment). And she appreciated that this one doctor didn't agree with the others. Which meant he was on *her* side. Maybe she could call Rain from his place. And maybe they could pick her up tomorrow on their way out of town. This turn of events could be just what she needed.

Certain she wasn't going to get a better offer of assistance, she clambered into the back of the van. As she got settled on the beanbag, with lots of room to stretch out her legs, the door slid shut.

"What's your name?" she asked. "I never really paid attention."

"Well, it would be pretty silly under the circumstances to call me Dr. Kempner. But I don't like my first name, so my friends call me Stop." Instead of doing another U-turn, he drove to the next light and made a left, heading around the block. From her spot on the floor, Lilly had a good view through the windows. Perhaps it was the candy in his mouth, but she had the impression that the whole van reeked of peppermint.

"Stop? That's kind of different."

"Trust me, it's better than my actual name." He gave her a wink in the rearview mirror. "It's a long story," he said, navigating away from downtown, picking up speed as they merged onto the highway. "Make yourself comfy, I live about forty minutes outside of town. Hungry?"

"Always." He tossed her a nut bar. "Thanks."

He turned up the music. It was a little too head-banging, and sounded more like screaming than singing, but it had a kind of thunder to it that made Lilly feel powerful. She nodded along, and met his grin in the rearview mirror.

"You're a cool girl, Lilly."

"Thank you." For the first time in a long time Lilly felt like maybe everything was going to be okay. She *was* a cool girl. And while she wasn't fully sure why Stop was helping her, perhaps his name revealed it: he was on a mission to stop the bad guys from carrying out their brain-carving experiments. It was easy to imagine herself with a jack-o-lantern head, an empty smile fixed in place after their tinkering went awry. Whatever his reasons, he was helping her get away. And *away* was where she needed to go.

LILLY

I t was an enjoyable ride, past farms with flowing rivers of cornstalks and pastures trampled by cows. She and Daddy had never done any long-distance traveling and the new terrain made her excited for everything she'd get to see on her journey. They drove in a straight line for a long time, and then finally Stop turned onto a smaller road. Soon after, he slowed and turned again, this time onto a steep and bumpy path that she realized was a driveway. At the top of the hill she saw a purple castle—a frosted gingerbread mansion, complete with a turret.

"Is that where you live?" she asked, awestruck as the magnificent place came into view. It had a huge porch that wrapped around the house, a hundred windows, and a pointy roof—like a dunce cap—that sat atop the round turret.

"Yes—but don't be too impressed. Long ago this was the home of some bigwig—he owned lots of the farms out this way. But just like the land got broken up into pieces, the house is apartments now." He pulled the van around to the side, where there was another entrance. A mishmash of mailboxes clung to the wall beside the door.

Lilly waited for Stop to release the sliding door, but first he got out of the vehicle and glanced around, and then unlocked the house door and stuck his head in—looking up toward what she assumed were a set of stairs. What was he looking for? The place looked deserted. Stop came back and pressed the keychain button that freed her from the back of the van. Knapsack slung over her shoulder, she followed him inside.

A pair of lovely golden birds chirped from the porch rail, "Stop, stop, stop, stop..."

He ignored them, but Lilly grinned.

"Oh," she said when he headed downstairs. She'd hoped—assumed—that he lived within the curved walls of the turret, because, as the most castle-like part, she liked it best. She bent over to keep from hitting her head as they descended into the basement, and for a second Lilly felt a twinge of unease. Was he taking her to the dungeon?

Stop stopped in front of a door, a key at the ready. The floor beneath them was concrete, damp in places, and Lilly saw a laundry room with a bank of washers farther down the corridor. A light blinked on and off above them and Lilly hugged herself, partly from the chill, and partly from the anxiety of her failed expectations.

"You live down here?" she asked stupidly as he unlocked the door.

"I know what you're thinking, but it's a big space, and we have a communal garden in the back. I'm trying to save money, so I can move to a bigger city and buy my own place." He flicked on a light as he went in.

Lilly hesitated before crossing the threshold. Stop locked the door behind her as she took in his strange abode.

He wasn't kidding about how big it was. There was a long open kitchen to her left, and a living room on her right that could accommodate four full-sized, slightly raggedy couches. The ceilings were surprisingly high, though there were only a couple of small glass-block windows. A few miss-matched ceiling fixtures illuminated isolated pools, leaving much of the room in shadow. The overall darkness confirmed her fears of its dungeon-like nature.

"There's a bathroom at the very end there if you need it," he said, pointing. "And my bedroom's over there, but I usually sleep on one of the couches. It's a bit gloomy in the bedroom, but if you're more comfortable in there you're welcome to it."

She started toward the bathroom, but stopped when she noticed the textured walls. Large swaths of wall—and even the ceiling—were covered with gray eggshell foam.

"Is this to soak up the moisture?" she asked, remembering the wet patches on the floor beyond his door. The floor here was also uneven concrete, though much of it was hidden by threadbare Oriental rugs.

Stop laughed. "Nice try, but it's soundproofing." He directed her attention to his oversized speakers. "I like my music rather loud."

Lilly nodded like it was all cool, and proceeded to the bathroom. His apartment was unique, but she knew she didn't belong there. Though only eleven, she recognized it for the party pad it was, and hoped Stop didn't invite friends over before she departed. Suddenly she felt very young, and even more lost than when she'd run helter-skelter away from the TV vans.

like your bathroom," she said as she came back. It seemed like a mile between the bathroom and the kitchen.

"Everybody likes that crazy tub."

"*I* might even fit in it."

He laughed his easy laugh. "You can try it later, if you want."

As Stop poured a gloppy mixture from the blender into two glasses, Lilly noticed the photographs spread across his table. She hovered closer to get a better look.

"Hey—these are me!" It was not a happy discovery.

"That they are." He didn't seem sorry at all. She thought he should've sounded at least a tad guilty, especially since half the pictures had nothing to do with her Case. Some were just shots of her leaving her house or walking into school.

"Why do you have these?"

"Because you're the most interesting girl in the world."

On another day that might have flattered her, but it was becoming super obvious that Stop was weird. His name, his apartment, his extracurricular activities.

"I made us smoothies—banana-strawberry. Sound good?"

They looked thick and fruity. Her stomach burbled. "Okay."

She reached for one, but Stop gestured toward the colossal living room, a glass in each hand. "Might as well relax. Do you want to call anybody? Your dad?"

Lilly thought about it. Her journey was in its infancy, and felt so precarious. It would be better to wait until she was a lot farther away before she called her dad. Stop was eccentric, but at least nobody would find her here.

"Maybe I'll call my friend later." She set her knapsack on the floor by one of the sofas, and pulled her red hoodie off.

"Sure." He wedged himself into the corner of a perpendicular couch. When she was seated he handed her a smoothie, and clinked his glass against hers. "To an amazing adventure. And an amazing adventurer."

He had a way of making her feel good about herself. "Thank you for helping me."

"I'm just glad I came along at the right time. You're an exceptional young lady, Miss Lilly. Unwind, put your feet up."

She kicked off her ugly shoes and stretched out. The sofa was l – o – n – g and she had ample room.

"Will you be mad if I fall asleep?" he asked. "I know it's early for you, but I was working all night."

"No problem." She took a big chug of smoothie. "Yummy!"

"Oat milk, bananas, strawberries, and my secret ingredient." He waggled his eyebrows up and down. "A squirt or two of chocolate syrup. Okay, maybe three."

She giggled, and gulped the rest in noisy swallows. Stop ogled her.

"Wow. You were either really hungry or really thirsty."

"Both." She set the empty glass on the table between the two sofas, the center of which was green glass etched with gold. All his furnishings looked like they came from an earlier century. "I have a pretty big appetite."

"I guess you do." He seemed pleased. "Can I get you another?"

"No thanks, I'm good." Good as in not hungry, but...

Something overcame her and she felt as if *she'd* been up all night and needed a nap. But she wasn't just tired—her eyes wouldn't calibrate and she was in a kaleidoscope, seeing the room in multiples. She blinked, trying to focus, but gave up and laid back on a tasseled pillow. "I feel really…"

Her arms were too heavy to lift. And she wasn't sure if the rest of her body was still attached. Her eyes could still move; she looked at Stop.

He looked terribly pleased with himself, his right ankle resting on his left knee. "I guess I got the mixture just right. Or maybe it helps to drink it really fast."

Lilly tried to ask a question, but her mouth wasn't working. Oh no! This was what her father had feared—that her heart would give out and her giant body would start to collapse. Stop set his glass beside hers and leaned forward, but not with the urgency of a medical professional whose patient was in distress. Even if he mostly worked with mice, he should have been able to tell that something was wrong. Yet all he did was gaze at her.

A noise gurgled in her throat, a wordless question.

"Feeling more relaxed?" he asked in a smooth velvet voice. The sound of it made colors in her mind. Burgundy. Emerald. There were too many teeth in his mouth, smiling at her as she lay within the tomb of her uncooperative body.

Heart attack, she wanted to scream. *Stroke.*

But Stop appeared unconcerned. Did that mean she was fine? Her eyelids became heavy weights, blinding her, even while her brain still clamored *What's going on?* Before she lost consciousness she wondered if he had tricked her, and if he meant to deliver her to the hospital, to the other doctors, after all.

LILLY

wareness came in fits and starts. Nonsensical tidbits seen from afar, as if she was watching herself on a movie screen, acting out the bits from a film Daddy would never let her see. She couldn't understand at first who she was with, or where she was. Then she remembered: Stop, and the drive to his dungeon apartment.

As he moved on top of her he growled like a rabid dog. The sound scared her; all those gnashing teeth, so close to her face. There was a delay before she felt the pain. Between her legs. Her brain wasn't functioning right and she desperately needed to understand, to put the puzzle pieces together...How had she become a paralyzed log of meat, being ground to shreds for the satisfaction of the carnivorous monster atop her?

And all at once she knew.

She was being raped. He'd drugged her.

At Rain's they'd watched part of a news magazine show more horrible than anything they'd ever imagined. It was about *this*. Having no control of your body. And being violated. The weeping cheerleader begged the interviewer for... What was it she'd wanted? They turned off the TV before finding out.

"Stop."

His eyes were clenched tight and he made his feral noises. She remembered drinking the smoothie in a few quick gulps. And then getting sleepy. But her eyes were open now and her hands and feet were tingling. She was coming back to life, and as her awareness returned she felt it even more, the hammering as he moved in and out of her.

"Stop!" she said louder.

This time he opened his eyes. He grinned his jackal grin, but slowed his thrusting only for a moment. "There you are. Less awkward to get started this way, dontcha think?"

"Stop!" she screamed as he ignored her protests.

Why was he doing this to her? He was supposed to help her. She thought he liked her, she thought he was on her side.

"Stop! *Stop!*"

"Yes, yes!"

Horrified by his pleased reaction, she tested the use of her arms. The right one flopped a little, but as she concentrated she was able to make fists with both hands. She urged her awakening blood to circulate faster; she clenched and released her hands, and wiggled her fingers about.

Stop heaved against her one last time, howling like a wolf. She screamed too.

Lilly got her left arm to work, and punched him in the face. He met her eyes, breathing so heavily that the peppermint fumes from his mouth filled her nostrils. But to her dismay he looked surprised and not injured.

As his breathing settled, a smirk shimmied onto his face. "You can't tell me you didn't enjoy that. I know you looked forward to the appointments every week, just so I could touch you. Now we finally get to be alone."

What? She'd *hated*—oh. Oh no! Stupid Stop thought she *liked* what she *hated*. Everything was backwards for him; she should've been crying out "Start!" Lilly gathered her strength, her coordination, and struck his cheek as hard as she could with her right elbow.

"Ooof." He tumbled onto the floor.

She swung her legs to the ground and sat up, unsure what to do next. He crawled onto his knees, a hand pressed to the side of his face. He looked as woozy as she felt, with his eyes bobbling around and his pants at his ankles.

When Lilly stood up she felt her whole body unhinging, lengthening, like her dad's folding carpenters ruler, which she'd played with as a kid. Standing tall, her denim skirt slipped back into place, covering her exposed legs. Gazing down, Stop looked so small, so insubstantial; it was hard to believe he was the source of the tearing pain that still throbbed between her legs.

Lilly didn't think about her strength before she kicked him in the stomach, she just kicked as hard as she could. He flew a few inches in the air, a limp rag, and landed with a groan.

"Why did you do that to me?" she yelled.

He squirmed, clutching his side, his face twisted in agony. "You broke my ribs."

All of her muscles came back online, and with them all of her rage. What sort of man was this, determined to hurt her one way or another—under the guise of being a doctor, or under the guise of a friend. She'd never known there were such people in the world, capable of many faces, all of them cruel.

As she stepped toward him he wormed away. A snarl twitched on her face and something poisonous dripped down the inside of her thigh. Her egg-yolk-yellow panties lay in a torn scramble on the rug. The sight of them made her even angrier, as if their ruin was her ruin; one fewer of the few items that made her feel normal. She registered her blouse, unbuttoned, but didn't stop to fasten it. Instead she tried to recall one of the few moves she'd learned before she quit taking karate lessons. None came to mind, though she wondered if she possessed the strength to chop him in half with the furious edge of her hand.

What did come to mind was a commercial—for a touring event of professional wrestlers. The word "wrestling" didn't fit the image of the brawny men in leotards and the way they bounced around the "ring" (also wrong, for something that was square). It had looked more like a circus act for failed superheroes. That's what she was going to do to Stop.

You can be mean if you have to.

Rain told her that. And now Lilly understood.

Stop stopped retreating as she stopped advancing; he lay on his back, hands protectively clutched over his tender abdomen. Lilly took two quick steps and launched into the air.

Stop's eyes grew wide and googly, but he didn't have time to roll away. Lilly landed butt-first on his midsection, just as she'd seen the wrestlers do in the commercial.

In the commercial, the squashing-wrestler always bounced away, as if his opponent were a trampoline, while the squashee-wrestler made a show of blubbering and flopping about. None of that happened when Lilly landed on Stop.

She didn't bounce.

And beneath her came the crunch of bones.

He didn't moan or bawl. His bug-eyes froze and a stream of blood dripped from his parted lips toward his ear.

Lilly knew she had killed him, crushed his heart, mashed his organs, pierced his lungs, and the only thing she regretted was how difficult it was to get to her feet while sitting on her flattened attacker. He was squishy like the beanbag in his seatless van. She wobbled off his torso and onto her knees. Once she was upright, she considered him.

Now what?

She had no idea what to do. She'd gone from being a runaway to a murderer. Should she dispose of the body? Alternately, she could call the police. Neither seemed like an especially good option. She had zero desire to touch him in any way, even to roll him in one of his rugs. And if she summoned the police they would blame her—she'd learned that much from the cheerleader. They'd be mad at her for squashing a Fine Upstanding Citizen to death and throw her in jail. And then the doctors would perform their barbaric surgery; they'd probably alter her personality on purpose to cure her murderous tendencies.

One day while sitting in the waiting room at the medical center she saw a slip of a girl dressed all in orange. It had taken Lilly a moment to notice the handcuffs, the ankle shackles—and the two guards who flanked her, both in bulletproof vests. Her dad nudged her, to stop Lilly from staring. But she couldn't fathom how that tiny girl was so dangerous that she required so much in the way defensive measures.

The police and the doctors worked together—and Stop was a doctor. No one was going to help her.

Lilly sighed. She felt unclean but not guilty. She felt sadness but no remorse. Stop ruined her chance to have

Rain as a travel companion—Lilly couldn't make her a fugitive too, an accomplice to her crime. Whatever happened next, she was on her own.

It was still fairly early in the day and her dad was probably looking for her. At least she could stay out of sight for a while, that's why she'd come here in the first place. She didn't want to touch Stop, but she also didn't want to see him. Using two battered sofa pillows, she covered his face and his disgusting parts. Then he looked like a smothered doll, with his arms and legs sticking out. Lilly retrieved her backpack, hoodie, and shoes. The ravaged underpants filled her with regret: some things could not be put back together. She balled them in her hand, stepped around Stop's body, and headed for the bathroom.

While the tub filled with hot water, Lilly threw the panties in the garbage.

At first the water hurt the tender spot between her legs. But the longer she soaked, the better she felt. The droplets of blood and muck dissolved in the water. It bothered her that there were parts of the attack she couldn't remember. What she did remember was bad enough, but the lost moments, the unknown, made her shiver even in the warm cuddle of the bath. More than ever she knew she was on the cusp of a great change. Maybe it had been inevitable from the moment she started growing that she couldn't remain who she was. Though at that time she hadn't envisioned the literal, physical journey that she would be required to take.

She dried off with a funky smelling towel, and put on clean panties, her boot cut jeans, the butterfly T-shirt, shoes without socks (she needed every millimeter of space), and finally, her red hoodie. Traveling clothes. She hadn't acknowledged it to her dad, but she was aware of her overnight growth; she always knew. The pain whispered in her sleep— *Ready for more?*—as she dreamt about the stretched-balloon sound of her bones expanding.

It seemed possible that she might never stop growing, not unless the people in the Village—the witches?—knew of a gentler remedy than the doctors of the regular world. She finger-combed her hair, crouching to see herself in the mirror. It surprised her how, in her eyes, she still looked like a girl, like Lilly, when it was ever more apparent that other people saw something else. Something that needed to be managed, or destroyed.

Back in the living room she turned on the TV and sat on the nearest couch. To her dismay, the local channels were running a streamer at the bottom of the screen: **Girl Missing!** They described Lilly's appearance and asked anyone with information to call the police. She saw her kitchen and her father's face. His eyes were red with tears and Lilly wished she wasn't the cause of his grief. She turned up the volume.

"...you can hear me—please, Lilly. Please come home. I'm so worried about you and I love you so much."

They cut to a reporter, hair whipping in her face as she stood in front of Lilly's house. "Authorities are hopeful that because of Lilly's..." She paused to find a word. "...unique appearance, she will be easily spotted and reunited with her concerned father." The reporter's voice continued as an image appeared—a recent phone pic of Lilly at her school desk, unaware she was being photographed. In the picture,

Rain was standing beside her, looking cheerful but ever so small. Lilly stared in awe: it was the first time she'd seen herself from afar, with another person beside her for scale.

She truly was a giant.

"Mr. Wolf says that in spite of her dramatic physique, his daughter's health is quite fragile and she was only hours from being admitted to the hospital to monitor her heart."

Lilly scoffed. Her *heart*. If that was true, running away wouldn't have been such a necessity. She flipped off the TV.

Everyone knew what she looked like now; she couldn't leave until it got dark. In the kitchen, she sifted through the dead pervert's photographs. There was one she really liked: Lilly the Giant with her tiny best friend, walking home from school. She folded it and tucked it in her back pocket; it was better than no Rain at all.

Forever hungry, she helped herself to Stop's refrigerator and made a sandwich piled high with fancy cheeses and tomato slices. Afraid the kitchen chairs wouldn't hold her, she returned to the living room to devour her meal. Her plan now was simple: after sunset she'd follow the country roads that led away from town, away from everyone who knew her height better than her face. What did she look like to them? Bigfoot? The abominable snow monster? Her size shouldn't have robbed her of her humanity, but it had.

She felt strong, in spite of the strain her heart was under, and in spite of Stop's unspeakable act. Perhaps she was delicate too, in ways that didn't show—in ways she didn't want to think about. Her journey was underway, and she had to keep going.

JAMES

It was growing dark. He worried the darkness would swallow his little girl, who was still but a morsel in a hazardous world teeming with insatiable dangers. If before he'd found some selfish reassurance in the thought of her absence from the house, now all he wanted was for her to come home. If only the moon, which they'd always enjoyed gazing on together, would extend its hand and show him where she was.

He understood her fear, her reasons for fleeing, and even his own failures—but from his paternal perspective her life was worth saving at all costs, even if there were side effects. And he wouldn't abandon the prayer that the growth process could inexplicably reverse itself. If one could grow beyond the parameters of human reality, wasn't shrinking a possibility too? He'd even be grateful for a Lilly who shrank *too* much—a miniature who could reside in her dollhouse. The smaller she was the easier it would be to keep her safe, so long as he tread carefully.

A police officer was still there—on the pretext of his helpful presence—but James didn't like the official scent he carried, the Worst-Day-of-Your-Life sweat that wouldn't wash out of his blue uniform. Nor did James like him occupying the space where Lilly belonged, across from him at the kitchen table. People were calling in unhelpful claims from all over the county: A mysterious giant had been sighted in a farmer's pasture, singing to his sheep; several witnesses reported a *tall girl* on a unicycle (or was it a girl on a *tall unicycle*?), speeding north as she clutched a large rabbit.

James thought it ridiculous when the officer asked if Lilly knew how to ride such an apparatus, or if she had a pet rabbit, but at least the press was gone now. The news alert was everywhere; the guilt-stricken navy-haired photographer had spread the word. When the doorbell rang the officer answered it while James stayed in the kitchen, wracking his brain. Where did Lilly believe the Village of Wrong Things might be? Had he joked about it once, when she was very young? Did he tell her it was near the North Pole?

"I wanted to drop this off for James, we're all praying for Lilly."

Recognizing Kendra's voice, James scurried to the door and found her holding a foil-covered casserole dish. He burst into tears.

"Oh darlin'!" Kendra pushed past the officer and guided James back to the kitchen. She slid the casserole into the fridge, and sat with him at the table, patting his hand.

"She's gonna be just fine—big, headstrong girl—this is just her way of saying she's unhappy, and then she'll miss her home and hurry back."

"I didn't know she was so unhappy," he wailed.

"Of course, you're a man, what can you understand about girls." She offered him a tissue and he blew his nose.

"But I've known her her whole life! We've always been a team, I'd do anything for her."

"Mr. Wolf?" The police officer hurried over, cellphone to his ear. "We have a possible lead."

James snuffled, quickly wiping his tears. "Yes?"

"A motorist reported seeing an exceptionally statuesque person in a red hoodie—"

"That's Lilly!" He squeezed Kendra's hand.

"I made that hoodie!"

"—get into a white van. They got part of the license plate and described a number of stickers, and we think it matches a vehicle belonging to a Dr. Traugott Kempner."

"That's one of Lilly's doctors!" He sprang to his feet.

"You see the power of prayer? God is good!"

As Kendra and James embraced, bouncing up and down, the officer finished his phone conversation. The skeptical part of James didn't think God deserved all—or any—of the credit, not when his daughter had been smart enough to hitch a ride with someone she knew. He didn't wonder in that moment why Dr. Kempner hadn't taken Lilly straight to the hospital (or home), or at least called him; he was simply glad she was safe.

"They'll send someone over to the address and report back," said the patrolman.

"What a relief!" James practically sang.

The mood became festive and Kendra retrieved her casserole and heated up plates of food. They sat together to celebrate—even the patrolman.

"What a scare she gave me," said James, shoveling noodles into his mouth at the rate of a man who hadn't eaten all day.

Kendra said a quick and silent prayer before she joined in. "It's a testament to how much we love our kids that they're so capable of scaring us."

"That's the truth," the officer agreed.

James, who hadn't realized how remiss he'd been before, asked Kendra about her own family. And the patrolman, Wesley, described his. Seated around the cozy table, swapping tales of parental close calls, James anticipated the imminent good ending to his own story. His daughter would be home soon. Given all she'd gone through, the stresses and titanic changes, he wouldn't even reprimand her for running away. He just wanted to wrap his arms around her (hopefully she wouldn't squeeze back too hard) and feel the throb of her heart, and know Lilly was back where she belonged.

LILLY

The moon tagged along behind her, illuminating Lilly's way down the deserted rural road. She had the impression that the world she knew had vanished and now she was walking in a new place. It was a comforting thought: she could be whoever she wanted here, not Lilly the Missing Girl or Lilly the Giant, but Lilly the Explorer.

The night seemed too quiet, absent of singing frogs or the insects who made instruments of their own wings. Her heavy footsteps echoed. At one point the distracted moon got too far ahead of her, then backtracked to keep lighting her way.

"Thank you," she said, glancing upward.

After what felt like many miles the road forked into two. Lilly wasn't sure whether to follow the left tine, or the right. She stood there for several uncertain minutes, until a hawk sailed past—a feathered plane, gliding low.

"Going, going, gone!" it called in a chipper voice. "And we have a winner!"

The hawk flew above the right branch of the road, so Lilly went that way too. Soon she came to an underpass enshadowed by the bowed heads of a long stretch of trees. The moon tried to dip down and light the spaces between the leafy branches, but nonetheless Lilly found herself in near blackness. It felt safe beneath the trees, as if their entwined limbs were protective hands who wouldn't let any more harm come to her.

When she emerged from their cover the lane turned silver and twisty, and no longer were there stretches of field alongside the byway. Her breathing became labored as she climbed a hill; from the top she stood in the berm and surveyed what lay ahead. The moon showed her endless treetops, and a perilously steep incline farther up the way.

Lilly couldn't see any route that would bypass the incline, and she questioned if she should've taken the left-hand road rather than follow the hawk. She worried about the stress such a steep hill would put on her busy heart, having become more aware of certain things that had previously gone unnoticed, such as her inner workings. Once-silent organs were now conversant, tap-tapping inside her as if spelling out a message. She wasn't sure what they were saying, but accepted it as a warning: she was growing too much.

She was running out of time.

Yet, she felt compelled to go onward. The moon beckoned and, like a wave in the ocean, she couldn't resist its charms. She vowed to take the distant hill slowly, taking breaks if she got winded. Plodding along, she contemplated "the witch with no spells". There were likely more residents in the Village of Wrong Things than when the poem was first written. If not a witch, someone else there might be able to help her, someone with unusual skills.

Now on a downward slope, with the incline looming ahead like the peak of a rollercoaster, a rumbling came up behind her—a roaring sound that fractured the silence. Abruptly the insects and frogs were in full voice too, as if the lull was the work of a remote control left on mute by mistake. Around their music came something more urgent and querulous, the thundering of something low to the ground. Lilly stumbled off the road and stood in the ditch, unsure what was coming. Something large, and moving fast.

Lights came up over the hill and she shielded her eyes, blinded by the broad swath of radiance. She still couldn't tell what it was; her first guess was a UFO. The glare passed her and the hulking machine squealed to a stop. Now the moon explained: a truck with a big red cab, and a trailer bed bulging with immense logs. The window rolled down. A dim bulb popped on and a bearded-face appeared.

"Hallo, lass—are ya lost?"

"No," she said, though the uncertainty in her voice had a flapping sound, like the moths drawn to her porchlight.

"Can I ask where you're headed? I don't encounter many folks in these parts."

He sounded friendly, spoke with a lilt, and looked like Santa Claus in the decades before his hair whitened. Lilly wouldn't be fooled: he might be hiding his true self behind that cheerful countenance. Yet, seeing how he was familiar with the nowhere through which they both traveled, he might have information.

"Can you tell me...I'm heading for the Village of Wrong Things. Am I on the right road?"

He made a sound like *ach* and scratched his beard. "Maybe lass, maybe. I haven't been there myself, but I know some ladies who likely know where to find it."

His mention of "ladies" encouraged her; ladies wouldn't

lead her astray. "Can you tell me how to find these ladies then?"

He puffed out his cheeks and exhaled, eyeing a distant road only he could see. "It's hard to give concise directions for traveling by foot. It's faster by vehicle."

"I know how to read maps," Lilly said hopefully.

The light inside the cab got brighter as he pushed open the passenger door and started rummaging in the glove box. "Might have one from when I first went to the Forest. The ladies are *near* there, I'm heading that way now."

The interior of his truck was decorated with bright fabrics and dangling doodads. Lilly stepped closer, intrigued by his collection of odd maps.

"Here, this one goes as far as the Forest."

Lilly took the map from his outstretched hand and unfolded it. And unfolded it. And unfolded it until her arms were stretched wide.

"Not many can hold that map just so," he said with approval.

A route had been highlighted in fluorescent yellow and it went around and around on itself, zigzagged, squiggled, backtracked. It looked impossibly long and Lilly's hope started to wane.

"It's too far," she said tearfully. "I'll never get there."

"As I said, it's much faster by vehicle."

In spite of what had happened before, Lilly knew what she had to do. She clambered into the truck and stuffed the map into the compartment with the others—and then reached out and pulled the passenger door closed.

"I need you to give me a ride," she demanded. Remembering her manners, she added, "Please."

"Oh lass, I don't think—"

"I *do* think! You're the only one who can help me."

He peered at her intently, as if *she* was a convoluted map, and the friendly smile fell from his face. What replaced it wasn't mean, but sad. He shook his head, tears in his eyes.

"I'm sorry for your troubles lass. No one should do you like that." Lilly pressed her back to the door, confounded by what he saw in her. "Do you know what I'm carrying here, on the back of my truck?"

"Logs?"

"Right. And if I took them anywhere else they'd be turned into paper or furniture. But I'm a professional thief, that's the truth. I stole these logs under cover of darkness, and I'm taking them to the Forest of All."

"What's that?"

"Perhaps...it may be in the vicinity of the village you're looking for. You see, the ladies I mentioned live in Town Town, which is on the other side of the forest. But the Forest is their domain, just as the mountains are on the other side of Town. I bring these mighty timbers to the Forest of All— these trees were slaughtered, they cry for justice. And the ladies plant them. It sounds impossible, I know—but they'll be trees again. The most magnificent trees you've ever seen."

Lilly believed him. She felt the truth of his words in her bones. "These ladies will know where the village is, I'm sure of it!"

"You're too young to—"

"It'll take too long to walk!" She prayed on the word *please.*

The burly man nodded. "I see your predicament. Okay. I'll drop my load at the forest, and drive you on to Town

Town." He released the brakes and resumed his journey. For the second time that day, she was in a stranger's truck. "And lass, on my word I'll get you safely to the ladies. And make sure no one else hurts you."

How did he know? Did she look different—had Stop left a mark on her that other people could recognize? She cocked her head and considered him. He was wearing a plaid shirt and blue jeans, there was nothing extraordinary about his appearance, and yet...Something told her he wasn't what he seemed, but in a good way. In an amazing way she didn't quite understand.

To trust him she had to trust herself, and her instincts were feeding her a sense of *certainty*. A *yes*. A *this is what I need to do*.

JAMES

It was almost midnight, way past Lilly's bedtime. Kendra was long gone. Michelle and Rain had stopped by—Rain gushing apologies. James couldn't concentrate. Dread was all he had, a rising, suffocating sensation, an unbaked loaf of bread plumping up out of control, stealing the space for his lungs.

It shouldn't be taking this long.

They should have brought Lilly home hours ago.

"What's going on?" he asked Wesley again. The patrolman had grown secretive—whenever his phone rang he stepped outside to answer it, and evaded James's questions upon coming back in. "Is something wrong?"

"The detective's coming to explain. He'll be here soon."

Detective. Explain. These were the wrong words. James paced around the living room, compulsively scratching his hair. It was probably standing on end, but he didn't care.

"Soon. Soon. That's what you tell a toddler who can't tell time. That's what you say when you have no idea. Do you understand what this is doing to me?" He sounded hysterical and with his hair all affright no wonder Wesley backed away.

"I'm sorry Mr. Wolf."

While eating casserole they were "James" and "Wesley," but with the deterioration of events—*the detective's coming to explain*—the officer had reverted back to hesitant formality.

Finally the detective came through the door, his skin as gray as concrete, and James almost laughed when he introduced himself.

"I'm Detective Harrison Gray." He was a cliché in a spartan suit, his demeanor as grave as the grim reaper.

"What's going on?"

"Do you want to sit?" the detective asked, the instant host in a house he'd never been in. James responded to the detective's authority and perched on the edge of the couch.

"Is she okay?" He wanted to get on his knees and pray. He wished Kendra was still there, to hold him up, to provide ballast against this somber professional who was sinking his ship.

Detective Gray sat too, angling himself toward James. In his presence James shrunk, a baffled child in need of the idealized patriarch who could tame the chaos. Wesley stayed by the front door, hands in front of him, deferential and ready.

"Mr. Wolf, I'm sorry we've kept you in limbo. We wanted to have a better handle on the timeline of events. When we went to Dr. Kempner's place his van was in the driveway and his apartment door unlocked. When we entered the residence...I'm sorry to say, we found him Dr. Kempner deceased on the floor."

James gasped, and the connective tissue that held him together started to disintegrate. "Lilly—is Lilly dead?"

"No, no. We don't think so. She wasn't there, but there were signs that she had been."

"What are you saying?" The disintegration process stalled, trapped in a murky nowhere, unsure whether to course-correct or finish its self-demolition. For hours he'd feared the worst, and then believed she was safe, and now he didn't know what to think. Were they back at the beginning? "Is she still missing?"

"I'm afraid so. Mr. Wolf, I don't want to keep the truth from you." Cracks appeared in his concrete forehead. "There were signs..."

Signs of what? Bad signs, or the detective wouldn't have hesitated. James's panic bubbled up again. "Is she hurt, did you find blood? Did someone kill the doctor so they could kidnap Lilly?"

"Not that." The detective pulled a plastic evidence bag out of his bulging jacket pocket. He unfolded it so James could see the contents. "Does this underwear belong to your daughter?"

James blinked. The torn yellow fabric came into focus but...There was so much fabric, they were so large. Nothing like the dainty little girl's panties he'd been washing for years. "I think so, maybe."

"We found these in Dr. Kempner's bathroom. He was in another room, partly unclothed. We believe...I'm sorry to have to tell you this. But we believe Dr. Kempner may have sexually assaulted your daughter, and she...She's quite strong now, isn't she? With her size?"

James nodded. Nodded and nodded. If he kept nodding his head would bobble off; already his eyeballs were coming loose.

"We think Lilly might have killed Dr. Kempner, and then ran—"

A keening sound ripped apart the room, a scream that couldn't squeeze through James's tightening throat. The patrolman hurried over and gripped his shoulders to keep him from tumbling onto the floor. James saw in his tearful eyes that he was Wesley again, a sympathetic father.

"Maybe not, you don't know..." James hyperventilated, the words a plea that would rewrite the past. He didn't want it to be true—that his daughter had lost her innocence, or that she possessed the ability to kill a grown man. "You can't...It's not..."

Wesley sat beside him, held him upright so the detective could finish.

"I'm sorry, I know this isn't what you want to hear. There were signs—based on things we found in the apartment...We think he might have drugged Lilly—"

"She's just a little girl!" James screamed. Part of him whispered, *A little girl in the body of a monster.*

"We've expanded our search; the news helicopters are helping. We consider it likely she's on foot, which gives us hope that she isn't too far ahead of us."

It was meant to be optimistic news: she was out there, alive, lumbering away at the speed of a behemoth. But a waterfall of red erased what James could see, or even think about. His child had been hurt (*blood*). His child had attacked her attacker (*blood*).

"How? How did she...kill him?" Did Dr. Kempner have a gun? Or maybe she grabbed a kitchen knife. But that whispering inside him knew. *She didn't need a weapon.* He felt her strength the last time she embraced him with her boa constrictor arms.

"Signs indicate... Your daughter's... very large now.

The coroner's initial impression was that Dr. Kempner was crushed, based on the condition of his torso."

The blood cleared from his eyes as James blinked. What the detective was saying couldn't be true. *Yes it could.* Lilly wasn't some boulder that rained down from the top of a mountain.

"Was it an accident?" James asked, still unable to envision Lilly with murderous rage.

"Maybe—if she wasn't sure of her own weight, strength. You don't need to worry, Mr. Wolf. Given the other evidence, that Dr. Kempner lured her, drugged and assaulted her, self-defense is..."

James tuned him out. The detective couldn't grasp his actual concern. Every instinct as a *father* told him to snatch the car keys, drive every street of every town until he found her. But every instinct as a *man* told him to lock the doors. And not let her in if she ever came back.

His worst fears had come true.

His daughter was a mutant. Grotesque. And deadly.

LILLY

As they chugged up the rollercoaster's gargantuan hill, Lilly was immensely grateful to be in Angus's comfy truck. Whenever Angus shifted gears, the mechanisms protested with grinding grunts and precarious yelps. Lilly thought she might have died while trying to walk this hill, and by the noises the truck was making, it had similar concerns. She peered at the mirror attached outside her window, wondering if the logs were tied down tightly enough to keep them from spilling all over the road.

"Know what you're thinking. We've crested this minimount a dozen times, and never lost a single timber." He grinned at her. "There's a turkey dinner with all the fixings in the cooler behind your seat, if you fancy a nosh."

For once she wasn't hungry. If anything she felt a little nauseated. "No thank you."

"Well, it's there if you need it."

She'd expected the road to plummet down the other side, but when they reached the apex she saw that its descent meandered in long, gradual switchbacks. Lilly could've sworn she heard the engine purring, like a great cat. Angus patted the dashboard.

"She's much happier now."

A short while later they came to a tunnel, burrowed through the side of a rocky mountain. The truck's headlights illuminated black curving walls that reminded Lilly of gelato, scooped out with a massive spoon. Only a short stretch of roadway was visible at a time, and there was no sign of the tunnel's end.

"It must be really long," she said.

"That it is. Quite long indeed. I won't blame you if you get bored of the scenery and fall asleep."

She thought he was joking. But on and on they drove through the slightly claustrophobic passageway. The view was so monotonous that, indeed, the longer Lilly gazed at it the more her eyelids drooped.

"Are we almost to the end?" she asked, trying to stay awake, and unsure how much time had passed.

"No, 'fraid not. I can switch on the overhead light, if you fancy reading a book."

"No, that's okay." It was a tempting offer, but she felt too tired to read. She hoped there wasn't any of Stop's sleeping potion lingering inside her. She felt safe with Angus, but it was better if she stayed awake and kept an eye on where they were going. Someday she might want to make the reverse trip, so she needed to know how to get back home.

Angus started singing a lovely but sad ballad; it made Lilly's goal of keeping her eyes open that much harder. No doubt it helped him endure the monotony of the endless tunnel, but the somber music nearly doomed her to the pendulous urge to sleep. Her chin flopped onto her chest, but she yanked it back up.

It flopped again.

And she yanked it up.

It flopped again.

And again.

And again.

Lilly was certain she'd resuscitated herself every time she blinked off to sleep. But daylight pierced her closed eyelids and she was forced to concede that somewhere along the way she'd taken a nap. The new terrain astonished her—the wide-open savannahs of a pristine continent, the sandy hue of the dirt road. But then something much closer caught her attention. Her hair was hanging in her face, significantly longer than it had been before they entered the tunnel.

Perplexed, she tilted her head downward to admire its full length, and then was startled by something else.

"Aaaaaaahhhh!" She tried to get away from it, but it was attached to her midsection.

It was right in the center of her, a rounded mound beneath her shirt. And now too short, the T-shirt rode up on her belly. The sleeves of her hoodie were above her wrists, her jeans above her ankles, and she couldn't wiggle her toes in the cramped confines of her shoes. By now she was accustomed to spurts that added inches overnight; it was her belly, big and round, that filled her with the terror of wrongness.

Had she developed a tumor? Is this what the doctors had called an ossification? Maybe it's what they'd feared all along, that eventually she'd start growing bits and pieces in wayward ways, and they would grow just as fast as the rest of her.

"Am I dying?" she shrieked, unable to process what was happening.

"Oh lass, you're all right. It's just the baby growing."

"The...?" Her brain shut off for a second. She scanned the terrain—maybe there was an answer out there. Scattered among the rocky outcroppings were incredible trees, with canopies that fanned out over thick, towering trunks. The sky looked pinkish and the colors everywhere were soft and plush. It was all very beautiful, but didn't resolve any of her questions.

"How far did we go?" *How long were we in that tunnel?*

"We're almost there now. Don't worry, the ladies will help you when your time comes."

My time? She gazed at her belly again. "Is that really a baby?"

Naïve though she may have been, she wasn't a doofus: with Rain she'd read *Are You There God, It's Me Margaret* three times. Lilly hadn't started getting her periods—it never occurred to her that Stop's attack could result in a pregnancy. She felt the rage of a wildfire. And betrayal beyond what her young body could hold.

This wasn't right. She was supposed to have a choice about these things, and she certainly wasn't ready to have a baby—but by all appearances it was too late. In the storm of her thoughts an even darker cloud encroached. Was Angus somehow responsible for this? Not for the baby itself, but for taking her through the not-an-expression-of-speech endless tunnel? He'd been through it before; he must have known how much time would pass.

"Let's go back!" If they went back through, maybe everything would reverse itself.

"We can't undo it, lass—and this is the best place you could be, I wouldn't have agreed to bring ya otherwise. The ladies will know exactly what needs doing—for the wee one, and for you."

She slumped against the door. "I don't want this, Angus."

She'd managed to stay reasonably content as her body grew, some aches and misgivings notwithstanding. And she'd even succeeded in quashing her rapist—quite literally—which she hoped would help her feel better about it, in time. But now it was all too much. Leaving home. Leaving Rain. Her life had become a firecracker, the kind with a bad fuse that took off a hand. She started to cry.

"Oh Lilly, it's not so bad, I promise ya."

"Everything's ruined! My whole life!"

"No, you'll see. At this stage of the journey it seems confusing because everything's so new." He spoke with such certainty, such compassion, that Lilly gave him her full attention. "You can't picture how it could possibly turn out all right." (True, she couldn't.) "But I *know* things. That's my payment from the ladies, because the earth owns the trees and it would be wrong to get money simply for doing the right thing. So I bring the trees, and the ladies bring them back to life, and they gift me with this special thing, this special knowing. And what I know about you..." He gazed at her for a long while, grinning in wonder. "I hardly have the words for the greatness you're going to be."

Lilly had never felt so special in her life. All the fine hairs on her arms stood up in approval to applaud. Her smile threatened to break through and wrap itself around her head. At once she felt both very small—a delighted child—and very, very important. She leaned over to plant a kiss on Angus's cheek.

"Thank you. I might've died out there without you."

"It's my honor, lass. And I'm getting ya there as fast as I can."

LILLY

illy thought there'd be a brown sign announcing the entry to a National Forest, like when she went camping with her dad. Instead, a vast woodland simply appeared up ahead on the horizon. When they entered the Forest of All she plastered her face to the window to take in the great trees. The sky above them took on the cheerful color of the happiest blue bird—a blue that rippled like the soft undulations of a gentle sea.

"Wow."

"They are a sight, aren't they?"

It was the strangest forest she'd ever seen. The trees were spaced in an intentional way that made it curiously unnatural, very unlike the hodgepodge of a regular forest with saplings of different ages, underbrush, ferns, decaying logs, shrubbery and whatnot. Here each tree had its own little area and rarely did the canopies appear to touch. The forest floor looked to be covered in mulch. Though every tree grew with abundant health, Lilly was reminded of the military cemetery—next to the regular cemetery where her mother was buried—and its tidy rows of headstones, a perfect line wherever you looked. It was like that here too, and by their arrangement Lilly understood that each tree had been *plant-ed*. None had sprouted through the soil like an ordinary tree.

Angus, cheery and relaxed, drove through the forest along a hard-packed dirt road.

"But how...?" Lilly needed a moment to formulate her question. She knew enough about ecology to know that different trees had different requirements—for light, moisture, temperature, even the insects and birds. "How can they all live together?"

"Oh, with a little help from the ladies. Someday—maybe soon—some of these beauties will be extinct in their regular habitats. They come from all over, I'm not the only one who brings them here. Sometimes I think of this as a zoo, a rehabilitation reserve for the great trees of the world—the last place they can live. The ladies know just what each needs to grow and thrive—or should I say re-grow."

"Is that why the light's so weird?" Lilly finally grasped the ripples in the sky: sunlight bathed the trees with varying intensity. Angus gave her a good-job nod. "Wow."

She meant that wow for the ladies. Not only could they bring severed logs back to life, they had the ability to populate the sky with made-to-order sunshine.

Angus pulled the truck into a circular clearing beside a large piece of machinery with a ginormous claw. He set to work using the grapple to unload the logs, and Lilly wandered off to explore. A pleasant shock came to her when she found the source of the chirping and tweeting, which seemed to emanate from the tree branches: the birds here made charming, wordless sounds, with pretty voices!

As she walked through the forest she saw trees she recognized, like the giant sequoia and the eucalyptus (which was the food of koalas). They were magnificent, towering over her, making her feel tiny—something she hadn't felt in a long time. As she approached a particularly impressive tree she realized it was a humungous version of the ones she'd spotted after awakening on this side of the tunnel.

"What kind is that?" Lilly called, pointing upward in case Angus couldn't hear above the clamor of his work.

"Isn't she a beaut?" He wiped his sweaty brow as he abandoned his task and joined her. "That's *andansonia gran-didieri*. The greatest of the baobabs, native to Madagascar."

It reminded her of a lighthouse. Tall, with a smooth trunk devoid of branches.

"It's like standing under the world's biggest umbrella!" The canopy was so far above them, spreading outward like a living roof. "Or, it looks like...The trunk is an arm, holding a bouquet of smaller trees."

That made Angus laugh, and Lilly giggled. Being among the trees made her feel so good. The air carried a scent so vibrant that the oxygen itself seemed alive. If only she could share all of this with Rain.

Angus started pointing to different trees. "Mountain ash, raintree, white oak, silver maple, hackberry, western hemlock, sacred fig, coast redwood, copper beech, scarlet oak, Sitka spruce, red cedar...You can see more, if you go in deep among them."

She gave him a look, questioning, and he immediately understood. "Safe as can be. I'll finish unloading and come find you."

"How do the trees—logs—get planted?"

"Oh that's not for our eyes. The ladies have their ways. I think they work at night, like me. I've camped here a few times, out among these wonderful creatures. And the next morning the timber I'd left by the truck was gone. Not for us to see.

"After I'm finished we'll drive into Town Town and I'll say hello, and you'll be on the next leg of your journey. Yeah?"

Lilly nodded, beaming with a happiness she hadn't felt...well, maybe ever. It would sadden her to leave Angus, but hopefully they would meet again. And after seeing the Forest, she was more eager than ever to meet the ladies. In a land so brimming with magic, the Village of Wrong Things might be just around the corner.

When Angus found her she was hugging a redwood. It was the size of a skyscraper, with a hollowed room at its base that she longed to make her own—if only she wasn't a pregnant giant on a mission.

"I wish we could stay," she said as Angus led them to the truck.

"The Forest of All is a part of you now, and you're a part of it."

He meant well, but Lilly desired more than a memory, more than philosophical sentiments. The Forest—like her home, her best friend, her father—was hard to leave behind. They drove up and over easy hills, while the liberated trees stood watch on both sides of the road.

The land changed abruptly and they entered a stretch of normal woodlands with roly-poly hillsides and trees that grew in untended chaos. Ahead was a clearing. And then they drove into a pocketsize town with the swagger of the Wild West about it—wooden buildings with swirling letters and fancifully painted façades. The town was surrounded by a mob of evergreens, eagerly waiting to be let in. They passed a cross street and Lilly saw houses of different styles and colors, no two alike. One of them had a wraparound porch and a turret that reminded her, even with its cheerful raspberry paint, too much of Stop's purple castle.

A nervousness came on, the runaway sizzle of butter overheating in a frying pan. Angus was sure the ladies could help her with the baby (could they help raise it too?), but what about her *bigger* problem? She couldn't live in the Village of Wrong Things (or anywhere else) if she couldn't survive her ever-increasing size.

Angus parked in front of a building whose wooden façade bore a two-story mermaid, larger than life, yet lifelike. The swinging sign read Yummy Things, which made Lilly think it was a bakery or candy shop. Three little old ladies sat in rocking chairs on the broad porch and waved and smiled as Angus got out of his truck.

"Hallo! Flora! Penelope! Doris! How are you lovely ladies?"

Feeling shy, Lilly wished she could huddle behind Angus. She hadn't expected the ladies to be so...wrinkly. Or shrunken. They looked too frail to do much more than rock in their chairs, how did they manage to care for an entire forest?

"How are you, Angus? Been a minute."

Maybe that was Penelope, the one in the middle—in pale yellow. They dressed monochromatically: the one to the left in light blue, the one to the right in orange sherbet.

"Good, doing well, always something to be thankful for."

The ladies nodded, pleased, but every scintilla of their concentration was on Lilly. She glanced around the town, uncomfortable with their scrutiny. As the ladies stood—not rickety in the least, but graceful—four more emerged from the store.

"We haven't had a need to gather in a long while," said the one in lavender, holding the door open for her friends.

"This is Lilly," Angus told them. "She's in need of some help, as you can see. She was looking for a village, but Town Town seemed like a good place to start."

"We can help her," said the little old lady in pink.

The seven ladies streamed off the porch, their movement unobstructed by the fragile bones or wasting muscles of the average elderly person. Lilly caught movement behind her and when she looked, more women were emerging from other storefronts. They weren't old, and some of them quite frightened her.

Seven were dressed in flowing robes in the hues of autumn, their long hair entwined with feathers and leaves. They were perhaps middle-aged, diverse in their size and shape and coloring, though each wore an amulet about her neck. The other seven were younger, tall and muscled, their hair either shaved or braided tight against their skulls, their faces inked with designs. These seven wore fierce gazes and each carried a weapon—spear, ax, a knife with a curved blade.

As they encircled her, Lilly tried to shrink into Angus's shadow.

"Shall I leave you to it then?"

Lilly wasn't sure who he was asking—the collective ladies, or her. She shook her head, but the robed women nodded. Angus gave them a little bow, and turned to head for—

"You aren't leaving me?"

"This is as far as I can take you. The ladies will care for you now."

Again, the women nodded—this time all of them. But Lilly didn't want to be left alone with so many strangers. With a friend at her side—Angus or Rain—she could've handled it. Rain was good with new people, but Lilly...On her own, she felt so very on her own. To bolster her courage, she took the photo out of her back pocket and snuck a look at Rain before pressing her against her heart.

"Don't fret child, we won't bite you," said a white-haired lady in a pale-gray pantsuit.

The women, all twenty-one, started closing the circle after Angus left it. Before he reached his truck Lilly ran to him, crouching down to give him a hug.

"Thank you, for everything."

"My pleasure, Lilly." He got in and closed the door. He looked happy enough, but tears stood in his eyes. "I truly can't wait to see you again."

"Me too."

He backed up, careful not to hit anyone, and drove out of Town Town the way he'd come. Lilly, not wanting to appear rude, or afraid (which she was), strolled back toward the congregation of women, with Rain's image tight in her hand.

They flowed into position around her, making Lilly the center of their circle. Seven little old ladies. Seven priestesses. Seven warriors. Lilly tried not to be scared, but the gleam in their eyes radiated something hungry. She was much larger than even the warriors, but Lilly didn't think she could take them all on at once, if they made a move to devour her.

JAMES

The steam from his coffee mug tickled his nose, trying to awaken him. Head on hand, he sat at the kitchen table feeling utterly worthless. His thoughts took up sides and fought a war he couldn't mediate.

She's fragile, vulnerable, your little girl.

She's colossal and capable of killing with her bare hands.

She needs you, she's alone.

You can't help her.

You love her more than anything.

Who is she...WHAT is she?

A good father wouldn't sit there doing nothing. A good father would be out with his parents and in-laws and the other search teams. A good father wouldn't make useless mental lists of the things he should have done differently.

1) Stayed home with her instead of going to church.

2) Had a talk about boys. And men.

3) Bought her a mothereffing cellphone.

4) Given the kid the damn hug she needed.

When Lilly was five and afraid of thunderstorms, she liked to make a nest in the bathtub with pillows and stuffed animals. She felt safe there, and James would sit on the fluffy bathmat and read her stories until the storms passed. It pierced him, like a power drill aerating his heart, that in her current size she was too big for a hidey-hole, a blanket fort, or any other place of comfort where she might seek refuge. He imagined her walking alone, mile after mile, and the image threatened to undo him. And yet…He was still sitting there.

The police said it was okay—that he could stay behind while they searched, in case Lilly came home. He couldn't admit to anyone that he was afraid of finding her, afraid of seeing her and what she'd become.

Only a monster would find consolation in imagining his child as a wounded animal seeking a quiet place to die—a hedge to huddle beneath, a church basement left unlocked. He didn't lack empathy. To the contrary, whenever he tried to calculate his own pain he remembered hers, on a scale so great it couldn't be measured. Her size hadn't saved her from being raped. He couldn't imagine what she'd suffered—in that moment, or the ones after.

Maybe she felt shame, or that she'd done something wrong. If only he could tell her he was glad Dr. Kempner was dead, though he wished *he* could've killed him. His teeth gnashed at the savage desire to rip out the pedophile's throat. If only James could've admitted—to Lilly, to himself—that some things couldn't be fixed. Then she wouldn't have left, and he could've spent her remaining days, however many there were, making her wishes come true.

Such sentimental thoughts for a man who'd promised his child unconditional love, and then reneged.

Go find her, she needs you!

She ran away from YOU, dinglehead!

The doorbell rang.

He took a gulp of coffee, unsure about answering it. It rang again. The jolt of caffeine triggered a reminder to get off his lazy ass.

It was probably a reporter, perhaps with an apology (to his shock, several had come by for that purpose)—or a neighbor bearing food. People were being nice and the least he could do was accept their kindness. When he opened the door it was Rain; Michelle waited in the driveway, the car idling. He held up his hand, the greeting of a tired robot, and Michelle nodded back, her face grim.

"Shouldn't you be at school?" he asked Rain.

"I couldn't. I really wanted to go looking for her, and Mom said I could but she's already super late for work. We, I...I was hoping, maybe we—you and me—could we look for Lilly?"

There were tears in her words and it shook James to the core, snapped him back to a reality where people were hurt by Lilly's absence and hadn't given up. He was the only person who ever forgot she was a blameless child, in need of love and safety regardless of...Regardless. Rain gazed at him, expectant, and he couldn't let her down.

"That's a good idea, I didn't want to go by myself," he said.

Rain grinned, and gave her mom a thumb's up.

"I'll have her home by supper," he called to Michelle. She looked happier too, and waved before backing out of the driveway.

He let Rain in and hurried off to his bedroom to tidy his appearance and put on his shoes. There was no reason for such excitement, but this—driving around with Lilly's best friend—suddenly seemed like The Thing To Do. The necessary action that had eluded him all morning while he stewed in his mistakes.

Minutes later they were on the road, Rain buckled in beside him, angled toward the window. They didn't talk much. He didn't know what to say to Rain, to comfort her, though he'd done his best the previous night to reassure her that this absolutely was *not* her fault. Without Lilly, they were missing the connective tissue that made their relationship exist. Who was Lilly's Dad without Lilly? He told himself it was better not to distract Rain, who focused on the scenery with the intensity of someone trying to puzzle together an elaborate sequence of code.

All the search parties started at Devil Kempner's place, working outward by foot or car. James pulled onto the berm across from the hideous Victorian mansion. Up on the grassy hill was a Crime Unit van. He and Rain gazed at the scene from afar.

"Is that where it happened?" Rain asked in a small voice.

James wasn't sure how much her parents had told her. He wouldn't have included the rumor of Lilly's rape; he still hoped it wasn't true. She might have clobbered Kempner before things got that far. "Yes. She was here."

"I'm glad she killed him."

He turned to the girl beside him. She looked older in her subdued state. Her eyes betrayed her difficult night, the shadows of her troubled sleep, the discolored aftereffects of tears. He'd always liked Rain, smart and loyal and spunky. Now he saw the killer in her, waiting—the part of her that didn't care about being nice. Did all girls have it? Would he have seen it in Lilly if he'd looked harder?

"I'm glad too."

Rain gave him a half-smile of approval.

If there weren't other apartments in the house, James might have set it on fire. Another of his useless musings. As the police continued gathering evidence from the devil's lair, James pulled back onto the road and headed onward. Lilly wouldn't have turned around, she'd have kept going in the most obvious direction that led her *away*.

"We'll be back in business soon!" he called over to Rain. "See, don't even need a tow truck."

"Okay!"

Rain sat on a moss-covered rock across from the ditch. Fortunately, he kept a stash of peanut butter crackers in the glove compartment, along with some juice pouches. Rain didn't eat as much as Lilly, but he'd been promising her a lunch stop for almost an hour (fifty minutes of which had been spent loosening lug nuts). Even before the flat tire, they'd made little progress in finding either Lilly or a place to eat.

The winding wooded road went on forever and several times James had suggested they backtrack and try the left branch of the fork; Rain urged him on. He couldn't imagine Lilly walking this far, especially without being spotted.

Rain thought she might hide behind a tree, so periodically she yelled Lilly's name out the window. She wasn't ready to give up, so they'd go a bit farther—as soon as he got the tire changed.

For now, Rain seemed happy enough with her snack, and he was pleased when the tire came off easily (unlike the lug nuts). Good thing, because his phone wouldn't get a signal and he'd had to abandon his original plan of calling for help.

He sopped his sweaty brow with the sleeve of his shirt. Just as he was about to retrieve the spare from the trunk, the woodland sounds were replaced by the diesel-engine roar of an approaching truck. Before he could wonder why he hadn't heard it sooner, the truck rounded the curve ahead of them and barreled their way. Since leaving the Scene of the Crime, he'd flashed his high beams at the few cars they'd passed, and asked through the window if anyone had seen a very tall girl. There wasn't time to leap into the car and signal, but Rain was one step ahead of him. From her rock perch she jumped up and waved her arms.

The truck squealed to a stop and a shaggy, bearded man hung his head out the open window.

"Ya need a bit of help?" he asked, his accent thickly Scottish.

"We're looking for my friend, she's very, very tall and her name's—"

"You mean Lilly?"

"Yes! Have you seen her?"

"Aye, would you be Rain then?"

James dropped the spare tire on his foot. He grabbed the crowbar and marched, limping a little, toward the hulking truck.

"What do you know about my daughter?" If this pervert knew about Rain then he must've spent time with Lilly. "Is she in there? Do you have her?" He climbed up the driver's-side steps, ready to crawl through the window. "Lilly!"

"Hold on now, you're Lilly's dad? Wait! Let me explain!" He held his hands up to surrender.

James had never seen anyone react to him with such fear, and it humbled him. He retreated, but still kept the crowbar raised as he gave the big man enough space to get out of his truck.

Rain, looking more brave than James felt, hopped off her rock and strode right up to the truck driver. "Where is Lilly?"

"I found her alongside the road—this one here, but farther back the way you came. She was troubled, and looking for a village. I wasn't positive of the whereabouts, but I felt I knew who would. Lilly begged me to give her a ride."

"You. Gave a lost child. A *ride*?" James sputtered. "And you never once thought to bring her *home*?"

The man took a step backward, his hands pleading please-don't-hit-me, as James advanced. "Sir, I don't think you understand—your daughter was in a pickle of a problem. I did what I could to help her."

"If you laid one hand—"

"*No!* Of course not! What do you take me for?"

James's brain hammered exclamation points against his skull. This bearded barbarian seemed earnest enough, if utterly stupid when it came to children and commonsense. A part of him still wanted to clobber the man, but he was the best lead they had in the search for Lilly.

"Why didn't she call me? Where did you take her?"

"Can you take us there?" Rain asked, calm and reasonable.

As the driver considered her his features softened. When relaxed, he looked less like an ogre and more...noble. Something hopeful brightened his face. "She spoke of you, on our drive. She hated leaving you behind, but she didn't want to entangle you in her troubles."

"She's all right then?" Rain asked.

"She's all right, for a girl who finds herself in an unexpected condition." He turned to James. "I couldn't call because I don't have a phone; wouldn't work here anyway. I took her to the ladies, I know they can help."

"Who are the ladies?"

"What's your name?" Rain asked, before James's question could be answered.

"Angus."

"Thank you for helping Lilly," she said.

This was the problem with girls: they couldn't figure out who to trust. Rain might be ready to believe anything Angus said, but James certainly wasn't. "I think we should call the police and have them take it from here."

"We don't need the police—can you take us to Lilly?"

"Yes, lass." To James he added, "But the police can't come where we're going—and before you get mad at me for it, it's not my doing. Some places are particular about who can visit. Lilly opened the door for you, a blood relative, and Rain would always be welcome."

"Let's go!" Rain sprinted toward the passenger side of the truck. There was no way James could let her go alone, but things were shifting in wonky ways and he didn't know what to do. This man wasn't making much sense, but what were the options? He looked back at his car.

"I promised Rain's mom I'd have her home for supper—is it far?"

"It's a fair way, but the return trip is much easier, a fraction of the time."

"Come on!" Rain climbed up and opened the door.

James still hesitated. Once he'd felt so sure of the minutes in an hour and the effortless rotation of the earth on its axis. Reality had become stickier with Lilly's unceasing growth. He half expected his feet to be too heavy to lift—or, if gravity changed the other way, he might drift off into the sky.

Nodding, he took the crowbar to his trunk, dumped the spare in, shut it tight.

Rain crawled onto the little bench behind the front seats as James got in the cab.

"Oh! This is Lilly's!" She held up a proportionally large red backpack.

"She must've forgotten it, me as well," Angus said, closing his door and revving up the engine. He drove forward until the berm was wide enough for him to turn around. Once they were heading the right direction, Angus turned to James, who felt as queasy as a man rocketing into space. "I think it's very fortunate our paths crossed, Lilly's Dad."

"James, I'm James," he mumbled.

"Her need was urgent, but the ladies understand such things. She's going to want you to see—and her friend as well—that she's going to be all right. More than all right."

Rain rested her elbows on the back of their seats so her grinning face hung between them. "Does that mean the ladies can help her stop growing?"

"Well, a person has to grow in the direction their life takes them, so it isn't about stopping her. But the ladies will help her settle into her best self, that they'll do."

And with that, they entered a tunnel. James felt himself sliding down the gullet of a long-throated animal. He wanted to resist, to fight, to question—to at least stay awake. The darkness was too tempting and the last word he uttered was "Who...?"

LILLY

illy slid Rain's photo back in her pocket. She took a deep breath and whispered "Hello," turning to acknowledge everyone. The twenty-one pairs of eyes studied her, but she noticed in their faces something friendlier than she'd first seen. A few of the warriors even started to smile.

Something sharp jabbed her gut and her first thought was a spear—but no, none of them had directed their weapons at her. She rubbed the spot on her swollen tummy and felt movement beneath her tight skin: a kick.

"Oh! It's moving!"

The robed woman with rust hair and faded freckles stepped forward. Ever so gently she felt for the contours of the thing growing inside Lilly. The movement of her hand drew a shape and Lilly had to abandon her denial: the shape was a baby. Kicking and growing with or without her readiness.

"We'll introduce ourselves," the rust-haired woman said, returning to her place in the circle. The warriors went first:

"Decembra."

"Alala."

"Phoebe."

"Camilla."

"Lissa."

"Roma."

"Neith."

Next came the robed women, the priestesses. "Emerald."

"Amethyst."

"Ruby."

"Opal."

"Jade."

"Beryl.

"Pearl."

And finally the little old ladies. "Penelope."

"Doris."

"Flora."

"Sibyl."

"Gertie."

"Brigit."

"Helene."

All were grinning and their warmth created the encouragement Lilly so needed. They emanated a thought as solid as a hug: *You're gonna be just fine.* Two of the littlest old ladies—Gertie and Flora—came forward and took Lilly's hands. She was at least twice their height (her jeans ever shorter) and when she tried to follow them her painful toes made her wince and stop.

"Take those off, dear. You don't need them anymore," said Gertie.

Lilly slipped off her ugly shoes and uncurled her cramped toes. She walked barefoot, the ladies leading her, and the ground was soft as a cushion. The procession headed for a church-like building, and Lilly didn't even need to duck to pass through the immense doorway. Once inside she gasped in wonder. The interior was unlike any sanctuary she'd ever seen—no pews or a pulpit, but a meadow of grass and flowers with butterflies flitting about. Slender trees arched toward the center like the buttresses of a cathedral.

"It's amazing!"

"We like it," said Flora, her eyes twinkling.

"Do you know where the Village of Wrong Things is?" Lilly asked, ever mindful of her mission.

"You aren't a 'wrong' thing, child, you have no need of such a place," Flora insisted.

"It's been ages since we gathered." Opal, the rust-haired priestess, gestured toward a wide stump of tree, intending for Lilly to sit. "But this will be a special one, and then we'll accompany you on your way."

"Where am I going?" Lilly sat on the stump, wondering what type of magnificent tree it had once been. She was glad they would guide her, but if not the Village then what was her destination?

"It won't be an easy journey," said Beryl, a squat brown woman with shells in her hair, "but you know that, and you're ready."

Lilly wasn't so sure. "Will you help me take care of the baby? I've never even held a baby."

"Many things will reveal themselves very soon, and you will know everything about who you are and what you were meant to be." Beryl clapped her hands twice and the room erupted with purposeful movement. The twenty-one women scattered, a practiced choreography, as they set about their tasks.

There came the dragging out of great bolts of cloth. The retrieval of baskets full of bread and vegetables. The distribution of clay bowls and cast-iron pots. Two of the warriors built a fire in the stone-bound ring designed for the purpose, and fitted a frame over it from which the largest pot would hang.

Captivated by the flurry of activity, a word came to Lilly—*cauldron*—and she wondered what the mammoth pot was for. Knives appeared, and wooden boards, and around her burst the sound of chopping. Turnips and leeks, beets and carrots, potatoes and celery. The designated choppers handled their knives with the proficiency of professional chefs.

As comfortable as she felt among Angus's mysterious ladies, Lilly had read enough fairytales to fear herself the main ingredient of whatever they were cooking up. Her fear became terror a scant moment later when three of the old ladies (their names were jumbled in her head) surrounded her, tugging off her shirt.

"What are you doing!" Lilly protested. But of course: they wouldn't cook her with her clothes on.

"Don't be a silly frog, everything you're wearing is too small."

"But—"

From the fire ring came the sloshing of water as it was poured into the cast-iron pot. Next, in splishes and splashes, heaping piles of vegetables were added, scraped off the cutting boards. The ladies followed the direction of Lilly's horrified gaze, and burst out laughing.

"You're not afraid of vegetable soup, are you?"

"Maybe she's never seen it made fresh before, you know how they are in the Other place, with their frozen blocks of food."

"Good, hearty roots, from the good, rich ground," said Penelope, joining the gaggle. "We wouldn't send you off without a proper meal."

Lilly's relieved sigh ruffled Helene's (or Sibyl's?) hair as she struggled with Lilly's shirt.

"Did you think we were going to put you in the pot?" Sibyl (or Helene) said with a chuckle.

"What am I going to wear?" Lilly wailed, hugging her chest. Even that didn't help, as someone snuck behind her and undid her bra.

"We'll make you something appropriate, and for now you can cover up with the quilt," said Gertie.

Just when Lilly was ready to burst into tears, ashamed of her nudity, the old ladies draped a hodgepodge quilt, big enough for a giant, over her shoulders. She'd barely clutched it closed when they started yanking off her pants.

"I could've undressed myself, you know—if you'd asked, or explained what was going on." She sounded as peevish as she felt.

Gertie looked at the others. "Huh. There's a thought. We'll try that next time—asking. Or explaining."

"Sorry, pigeon. We know each other so well sometimes we forget to talk. We're just so used to working as a group, everyone aware of their task." Penelope patted her shoulder with a hand both gnarled and strong. "We meant no harm."

This time, they asked for Lilly's underwear, which she slipped off discreetly from beneath the quilt.

The old ladies sewed huge swaths of buff-colored material together. It wasn't obvious what it would become, though it certainly looked large enough to keep her—and her expanding body—covered. Lilly considered her gibbous belly. A baby. *Her* baby.

She used to wish for a little brother or sister—would it be like that? Would it look like her? Or would she only see in it the snarling face of the evil doctor? It had all happened too fast and The Baby felt so separate from her, and yet here it was, growing rapidly inside her. *We're alike, then*. Growing in ways that shouldn't be possible. The thought caused an abrupt shift in her feelings. She wrapped a protective arm around her midsection.

Instead of worrying on it further, she watched the activity around her. A priestess tossed herbs into the soup, while a pair of warriors took turns stirring it with the heftiest wooden spoon Lilly had ever seen. The other priestesses sat close together, doing something with a handful of colorful stones. At first Lilly thought it was a game, but their expressions were too serious for that. One of the warriors sat on a stump near the doorway, whittling a narrow tree trunk. The others stayed in a cluster, grinding and mixing things in the smallest of the handmade bowls.

"Does anyone need any help?" Lilly asked. It felt wrong to sit idle while everyone else worked.

Her question only earned her a few smiles and a faint "She's a sweet pigeon," from Penelope.

When the warriors approached with their little bowls Lilly grinned, thinking they were taking her up on her offer.

But no. Decembra—her muscles as formidable as her ax—explained, "We will give you the markings of your journey. The girl. The fighter. The traveler. The mother. The mountain."

"Will it hurt?" Lilly asked. Up close, she could see that their faces were decorated with a combination of paint and tattoos. Tattoos meant needles.

"No pain, little mother. Only brushes. And fingers." The young warrior smiled and whispered, "Alala," to remind Lilly of her name.

"Thank you," Lilly said, mesmerized: Alala appeared to be only a few years older than she was.

They set about dabbing colors and stripes and dots around her face. Lilly shut her eyes; how good it felt to be painted, how tender their touch.

"Your belly now, little mother," Alala said.

Lilly struggled with the quilt, trying to expose her tummy while keeping everything else covered. Decembra helped, folding the fabric around the nearly-full moon of Lilly's child. *My child's in there.* The mound looked alien to her eyes, with stretch marks that could have been the dried riverbeds of another planet. The warriors resumed their work; the light tickle of their brushes was a balm against an ache Lilly hadn't much wanted to examine. For eleven-and-a-half years her life had proceeded at a certain pace, in a certain way. Her growth altered everything, and now the changes were coming too quickly to process.

When they finished, Lilly pressed her chin to her chest and studied their artistry. Black tendrils. Rose-colored shapes with meanings that eluded her. But she sensed something—even from the facial markings she couldn't see:

these were powerful symbols and they fed her soul.

The priestesses came over to investigate—and give their approval.

"Good," said Amethyst. (Lilly finally made the connection between the amulets and the priestesses' names.) "We're ready for soup."

Again, Lilly wanted to help, but they urged her to stay where she was. Gertie brought her a large wooden bowl and set it, deliciously hot, on her palms. The aroma rising from it was arousing and rich. Lilly's stomach grumbled and it was all she could do to wait for the twenty-one women to serve themselves and settle in around her. This time she wasn't in the center, but part of the circle alongside her extraordinary hosts. Emerald, the dourest of the priestesses, made a brief blessing of thanks, and everyone dug in.

The warriors gobbled their soup greedily, slurping and clacking their teeth on their spoons. Lilly felt the same hunger, and the soup brought warm happiness to her insides. The vegetables were tender, but with a hint of resistance, and they tasted nothing like what she'd anticipated. Instead of a recognizable flavor, each bite triggered a word.

Thankful.

Strong.

Earth.

Endurance.

Rock.

Power.

River.

Love.

Eternity.

How could a soup taste like such things?

As she gazed on her companions, each absorbed in their own sustenance, Lilly wondered if they tasted the same words, or were they each experiencing their own flavorful interpretations.

Jade, with her large, carved amulet, pointed a finger at Lilly as if she'd just won a prize. Once Lilly might have thought it outlandish that someone could read her mind, but not anymore—not since meeting Angus and traveling to...wherever they were.

When they were finished, the entire cauldron consumed, the warriors collected the bowls (again refusing Lilly's help). The old ladies brought forward their finished garment—it took all seven to carry it. Lilly thought it resembled a sand dune.

This time, instead of stripping off her quilt, Flora politely asked her to remove it. Lilly hesitated; everyone was looking at her and she didn't want to be naked for even a second. Opal and Beryl stepped in to help. While Lilly pretzled her arms and legs, the priestesses lifted the quilt and the old ladies swiftly draped the new garment over her, directing her arms through the designated slits. They buttoned the front with big wooden toggles and loops made of rough-hewn rope.

Roma, the warrior who'd been whittling the long pole, presented her with the finished gift: a sturdy walking stick, fit for a giant. Lilly stood for the first time since she'd entered the church.

Her joints creaked. Her back felt stiff, like the dried pages of a book forgotten in the rain (a mistake Lilly only made once). She rose and rose, soaring upward like a construction crane reaching for a faraway roof. She wasn't sure how much she'd grown while comfortable in the ladies' meadow, but it was a lot. The voluminous garment enveloped her, stopping below her shins, with long openings for her arms and ample room for her to grow.

What do I look like? Face painted, taller than ever. She was double the size of the warriors now. The baby did a happy somersault and for the first time Lilly smiled at the thought of having a companion.

"Are you ready, pigeon?" Penelope asked.

The word "no" quivered on her lips. Then Lilly remembered the things she felt while eating the soup. *Thankful. Strong. Earth. Endurance. Rock. Power. River. Love. Eternity.* And they were within her. Around her. *Her.* She'd grown into herself, and had never felt so strong, so powerful, so thankful or full of love.

"I'm ready."

The twenty-one women escorted her out the back doorway, which had appeared to be a hedgerow. Lilly touched the leaves on the ceiling as the tree limbs kissed her goodbye. The landscape beyond the backdoor was entirely different than the terrain through the front. They were at the mouth of a valley, nestled between rising mountains. It didn't surprise her (such was her acceptance now) that the colorful mountains were unlike any she had ever seen, each created from a different kind of rock. Reds, browns, pinks, grays. A geological oddity. Some sparkled with ribbons of bright minerals or veins of colored quartz, visible even from afar.

Though Lilly still wasn't sure where she was going, she felt a connection to something out there on the horizon, and the ladies were more trustworthy than the beating of her own, ever-expanding heart. They walked solemnly on either side of her as they left Town Town behind.

LILLY

While the path through the valley wasn't strenuous, Lilly was grateful for the walking stick. Her body moved differently now. It wasn't just the baby inside; her limbs were getting heavy. She felt her blood thickening, a syrup sludging through her veins. Could that mean her heart, too, had almost completed its journey?

"If I die," she asked them, "will you take care of my daughter?"

"They'll be no need for that," Emerald said with gentle confidence.

"You'll do just fine." Opal gave her the wisest of smiles and Lilly felt a surge of real *excitement*: the baby inside her (she was sure it was a girl) was all *hers*. It belonged to no one else, and just as Lilly had defied expectations, so would her daughter.

Halfway down the vale they turned eastward to cross the first ascending slope. The peaks looked too steep to traverse but Lilly didn't worry on that; they would find a way. A glowing sun beamed down on her, and butterflies swirled about, chasing each other in a game of tag. The procession walked without speaking but the wind whispered in the tall grasses—an invocation that Lilly could almost hear.

When they reached the base of the mountain range the sun remained high above, as if time, busy elsewhere, hadn't kept pace. The procession stopped and the ladies clustered around Lilly. Judging by the distance between her eyes and the tops of their heads, she'd grown during the walk. Her belly stuck out too far to see her feet, and the hem of her cloak brushed against the back of her knees.

"We'll take leave of you here," said Flora, indicating her fellow old ladies. "But the others will keep on."

Penelope reached up and held her finger. "Goodbye pigeon, you've been a delight. So glad we could share this part of the journey with you."

"Farewell my dear," Gertie said, so small beside Lilly. "We'll visit you often." All of the ladies nodded, excited at the prospect. "What a treasure you are, truly."

One by one the little old ladies wished her well, gripped her fingers, and told her they loved her. As they retreated across the valley, Lilly knew not to be sad: she would see them again, as promised—and she was feeling an urgency. Her destination beckoned.

The fourteen remaining women—the priestesses at the front—continued up the mountain. Lilly's bare feet were so solid she couldn't feel the rocks poking against her soles. They headed up long switchbacks that zigged, then zagged, across the face of a gray-striped escarpment. The view made her marvel—the distances she could see in all directions, and the treasures she found tucked into the rocks near her head. Delicate blooming flowers, and nests of newly hatched birds, tweeting their hellos.

At one very steep section they crossed over a lower

point in the rocky range, and left the valley behind. Now Lilly saw how deep the mountains went, and how varied in colors and geology and even, she supposed, habitats. Some peaks were topped with snow, others were awash in rich jungle greens. Where the Forest of All maintained an individual ecology for each tree, here there were the worlds that thrived on a multitude of distinctive mountains.

They descended a trail and came to the base of a hill with a terrain Lilly hadn't yet seen. It was sandy colored— not unlike her garment—and the boulders were flattened and stacked, with stripes of erosion on their rounded edges. Shrubs and pine trees sprouted between the sculptural rock formations, and the ground felt inviting on Lilly's feet, soft as velvet.

As the procession stopped, a savage pain tore through her midsection and she half-expected her bulge to break apart and tumble off like an avalanche.

"Getting close," said Beryl.

"This is where we leave you," Decembra said, indicating the warriors. "But the others will keep going."

Once again Lilly was showered with love and goodbyes. Her cloak was up to her thighs and her hands too awkward to reach, so the warriors gave the back of her calves a hearty pat, the farewell of comrades. They, too, promised to visit often, and reassured her she would never be alone. Again, she felt only gratitude for the shared part of their journey, and no sadness as they went their separate ways. Her very perception of space was changing, and a great excitement welled inside her as she tasted a welcoming with each cool inhalation of air.

Another pain came. Lilly clutched her great belly and

hunched over, breathing out gusts that stirred the soil at her feet.

"You're almost there, Lilly Wolf," Opal said, her rust hair billowing.

When she was ready, Lilly gripped her walking stick, nearly a cane now in her great hand, and shuffled onward, up the dusty, pine-speckled hill. The seven priestesses let her lead the way, and they followed slowly behind. Her legs, her body, her baby felt nearly as solid as the boulders around her. The strange sensations within her blotted out everything else. Her daughter punched against her insides, demanding to get out.

"Soon, little one," Lilly said, rubbing her baby's fist.

As Lilly climbed the hill, one heavy foot after another, she abruptly lifted her eyes—and there was her destination. The distance might have been as small as a step or as great as a mile, she could no longer gauge with accuracy using the measurements of her previous life. The certainty of her journey's end gave her a renewed energy to reach it. To claim it. To tumble into the comforts of her very own abode.

"We'll wait here," said Beryl, and the priestesses nodded.

"You're almost there, brave girl."

"You'll know what to do."

"We're here if you need us."

"Oh Lilly Wolf!"

"Be the greatness you were destined for."

"You are, and always were, the everything."

Clutching her enormous belly, Lilly dropped the stick and used instead her powerful arm, limping apelike and alone up the final switchback.

JAMES

Angus blathered on about the forest, but James didn't care—wouldn't even look at it as they drove through. "Can we stop and walk around?" Rain asked.

"No." Even to his own ears his anger was a gunshot, but after they'd emerged through the endless tunnel Angus filled them in on Lilly's *condition*. James wanted to leap out of the cab. He was sure he could outrun this bumbling truck in this misfit forest and Lilly needed him and how could she be *pregnant*—about to give birth! He had no choice but to stay in the truck and he hated not having choices—but he couldn't send the shrapnel of his fury into Lilly's innocent friend.

Angus, on the other hand...If Rain weren't in the back-seat, James might have strangled the bearded Scotsman, chucked his body out and driven the rest of the way himself. No, Angus wasn't innocent in this, never mind his protests that he was *helping*. A grown man didn't drive an eleven-year-old girl *away* from her family, away from the known world. Where the hellfire were they?

Finally they left the wacky forest and entered a wood-land that looked more normal. Angus shot him nervous glances. "Almost there."

And then they were out of the woods and in...Well, there wasn't a welcome sign, but it had to be Town Town—a ridiculous name for a ridiculous place. Angus had brought his child to a lunatic asylum and James would never forgive him. The buildings were little more than ramshackle hovels and as the brakes screeched, spitting up dirt, the lunatics emerged to greet them.

James was first out of the truck. A gaggle of shrunken old ladies, dressed in church clothes, toddled out of the candy store.

"I'm here for Lilly." He struggled to maintain eye contact with them. He'd expected dazed, milky cataracts, not this sharp, scrutinizing gaze. As Rain joined him, the little old ladies shifted their attention. Their wrinkly faces crinkled even more as they smiled.

"Hello!" said Rain. "Have you seen my friend?"

"Such a wonderful girl!" said the crone in chick-yellow.

"You must be Rain," said the one in a synthetic coating of Pepto-Bismol.

"Where is she?" James demanded.

Again, the old biddies found something more interesting to look at, and James turned to see what had distracted them.

He stumbled backward. Seven armed heathens stalked toward him, their faces like tattooed savages, eyes murderous, weapons raised.

"Who brought you here?" one of them bellowed.

Angus stepped out from beside the truck, demurely waving a finger. "It was me, Decembra, sorry. It's Lilly's dad, so the door was unlocked."

The savage turned to address the old ladies. "We really need to fix that door."

The old ladies shrugged and nodded. "Maybe when the rest get back," said the one in sickly blueberry.

"Look, I don't want to be here anymore than you want me here. I've come for my daughter. Just show me where she is and I'll be on my way."

But instead of getting an answer, the heathens came closer, their eyes on Rain. Bless her heart, she had no awareness of the danger they were in and James felt an obligation to protect her. But before he could put himself between them, Rain smiled and met the savages halfway.

"Hello, I'm Rain! Thank you for helping my friend Lilly!"

The armed women looked like they wanted to eat her, their smiles salivating as they encircled her.

"She's our friend too," said the heathen with a curved knife.

"You look different from your photograph," said a girl with a spear.

"Is she okay?" Rain asked. "We've been so worried about her."

"Better than okay, young friend." The old ladies surged forward, scurrying with surprising speed.

The ancient ladies and the savages started escorting Rain across the road, toward a ruin with a massive door. Realizing they meant to leave him behind, James jogged to catch up. He looked back at Angus, who casually leaned against his truck.

"I'll stay. Take ya home when you get back."

Back from where? Michelle was going to kill him—they were already late for supper, his phone wasn't working, and if these crazy women did anything to Rain she'd never forgive him. Only a true idiot would lose someone else's daughter while searching for his own.

One of the heathens snarled at him from the doorway and he was afraid she wouldn't let him inside. But she did. Her breath smelled like decomposing rats.

"Oh wow!" Rain said, goggling the floor, the ceiling, the nothing.

James wasn't impressed. Tree stumps. A garden. A large cauldron forgotten over a dead fire. It looked like a witch's abandoned fort. Two of the armed women kept close to him, watching him the way an amused cat kept its eye on a mouse it wasn't quite ready to kill.

"Have you always been called Rain?" asked an old lady in the flesh of a cantaloupe.

"Of course!" Rain said. "My mother is very into nomenclature."

"It's a good name for a warrior," said one of the armed women, who, James had to concede, might indeed be a warrior. That they'd trained with those weapons was a worse thought than if they were punks who just liked to look dangerous.

Rain ran to a huge stump, upon which was a crinkled photograph. "This is me and Lilly! She really was here—look!"

She handed James the photo and he took a shuddering breath. It was tangible proof. This nightmare was real. When Lilly's growth spurt began he hadn't known they'd entered a slipstream, and would be pulled deeper into the phenomenal with each passing day. More than anything, he wanted *out*. He wanted out even more than he wanted to find Lilly. But he needed to finish this chapter. An understanding dawned on him: if he found her, if he successfully completed his mission, *everything* might return to normal. Wasn't that how such stories went, a reward for enduring a life-changing trial?

The youngest warrior held her spear for Rain to examine. She touched the carvings on the shaft, her eyes aglow with awe as if she'd been shown the key to a magical kingdom.

"This is ridiculous. Angus told me—" James stopped. Fourteen heads (fifteen, including Rain) snapped their attention on him and he reconsidered acting like a pissy tourist. Courtesy, even fake and forced, always brought better service. "Lilly's in trouble and I have to get to her, she needs a doctor."

The old women scoffed.

"Doctors, what do they know," said the Pepto lady.

"She's having a *baby!*" he shrieked. Screw courtesy, lunatics couldn't be reasoned with.

"She's not the first. The female body is designed—"

James guillotined the lavender freak's words, not in the mood for a lecture. "She's *eleven!*"

"Well, twelve. Twelve now," the sick blueberry said. "Time works differently here."

"I'm three months older than Lilly, so am I twelve too?" Rain asked, obviously hoping she was.

"Why yes you are."

He clenched his teeth. "The point is she's a little girl. Who needs help."

The warrior whom Angus had called Decembra planted herself in front of him, too close. She stank of skills he didn't have. Surviving a war. Plotting revenge. "You have no understanding of your daughter. Fortunately she came here. We helped her."

"She's fine, Mr. Wolf." The chirpy one in pukey green waved her hand dismissively.

James couldn't fathom their lack of urgency. "She's alone!" he thundered.

All fourteen of the lunatics laughed, uttering a chorus to contradict him.

"She's far from alone."

"Who do you think we are—"

"...never leave a *child* alone—"

"...no *clue* who Lilly—"

"...this is why we don't let—"

"Gotta fix the door."

As quickly as they'd erupted, they fell silent. The silence lingered for an uncomfortable spell during which everyone gazed at him. James refused to feel wrong for caring about his traumatized, ill, suffering, young child. None of these kooky, flippant women could be trusted, but he had to calm himself: rushing them wasn't producing results.

"I'm sorry, I'm sure you're all...well intentioned. But Lilly's been gone for...I don't know, time is—as you said—confusing. I made mistakes, I know that. I want Lilly to know I'm sorry, I want her to know how much I love her, I want to take care of her—"

"Lilly has needs beyond what you want."

To his shock, the words came from Rain. She looked at him with a gravity that defied her eleven—twelve—years.

"We were going to give you a meal," said the chick-yellow crone. "Not a gathering, as we gave Lilly, but our simple hospitality. There's no hurry, the others aren't back yet. But I suppose we can skip the niceties and head out. If that suits you better."

James hated how they'd turned him into a bratty schoolboy. He didn't understand what was happening, where they were supposed to go or who these "others" were. But if it led him to Lilly and the completion of his mission... "Thank you, yes."

The fourteen abominable women headed toward a giant hedge. Sunlight poured in as they pushed it open.

The youngest warrior fell in beside Rain, handing over her spear. "Doubles nicely as a walking stick."

Rain thanked her, and gave her a little elbow nudge like she used to do with Lilly. Girl code: buddies. She glanced behind where he was bringing up the rear, and in her eyes were questions. And disappointments. And accusations. He almost felt Rain begging him *don't mess this up*. As if all he had ever done was mess things up.

LILLY

The pain built inside her and she needed to scream. But she held it in—she wouldn't reward herself with the relief of her voice until she was there. A step. Another step. It was tempting to succumb to the agony and crawl on her hands and knees, but a greater desire kept her upright, and not simply the dignity of it. She wanted to admire her domain from her full vantage point.

She reached the apex of the hill and stood tall, though it hurt every part of her to do so. Something cracked: her spine, breaking. But she didn't need bones anymore. From here she could see all the mountains to the east, and the indigo blur of an ocean on the horizon. Turning westward, there was the valley—and there, in miniature, the church. Beyond Town Town lay the Forest of All, with its necropolis of eternal trees.

Southward she saw a tangle of distant roads, gray yarn looping around itself in wayward chaos. It took the people there so long to get anywhere, trapped in their circuitous travels. Such thoughts made Lilly feel sorry for them, and glad she was home. Turning northward she saw the solar system, the great road of the Milky Way, the planets hovering like moons.

Down on the path from which she'd ascended she spotted the seven priestesses, little bigger than insects, watching her. Waiting.

She blew them a kiss; they would feel her in the air.

A great ache howled its impatience and Lilly could contain it no longer. It came from all directions, as if she'd swallowed a thunderstorm; the bolts of lightning threatened to cleave her. Lilly took in a great breath, a breath like the winds of a hurricane, a breath that emptied the stratosphere. She screamed the tornado of everything she'd ever felt—the pain, the joy, the confusion, the dreams.

She screamed for her father, and for the mother she never knew.

She screamed for the brute who'd taken something that wasn't his.

She screamed for the friend who was like a sister, the guardian of her spirit.

She screamed for her childhood. For the trajectory of her incredible life. For the triumph of who she was.

She screamed for the miracle of her journey. She screamed for the first man who fully saw her. She screamed for the ladies—all twenty-one. All one trillion. All infinity.

She screamed for the forest, and the sky, and the animals. She screamed a home for them on the vastness of herself.

She screamed for the baby that wriggled out from between her legs.

She screamed her daughter's name in the language only the two of them spoke.

She screamed until she was finished, until nothing was everything, until empty was full.

Lilly took the bundle in her arms and her daughter's cries blended into the cacophony of her own tremendous noise. She held the baby against her heart and uttered one final bellow...

The impossible sound of the largest mountain.

Long after she fell silent, Lilly's transcendent cry reverberated against the stone bodies of the surrounding peaks. In this way she introduced herself and her daughter, and the neighboring mountains rumbled a greeting in reply.

She rested then, the baby in her arms.

JAMES

James kept his thoughts to himself. To say anything was to earn the laughter or hostility of the women with whom he walked.

When they reached the other side of the valley the old ladies begged off and left the warriors to take them the rest of the way. He wasn't sure why they opted out; even if ancient, they seemed fully capable of climbing a mountain. If Rain hadn't been there, he might have feared the warriors intended to chop him up and feed him to the vultures.

They climbed the switchbacks and periodically a foul-smelling warrior turned around to ask if he needed a rest. Though he was huffing for breath, he'd never admit to his matronizing entourage that he was struggling. Even the way they walked—jaunty in step, as if out for a leisurely stroll—was an intentional stab to his ego.

Often he wanted to turn back, run across the valley, and find his way back to town—to Angus, to the truck, home. He had no sense of his daughter in this strange place. Had she really passed through here? Walked these same trails? He felt so out of his element and he couldn't rule out the possibility that this was an elaborate trick. Perhaps, in some manner, they'd swallowed Lilly, and planned the same for him and Rain.

He wished Lilly had left more clues, like the photograph, so he could find her and finish this. Nothing here related to Lilly, except possibly Rain. But she was getting so chummy with the heathens that he feared she wouldn't want to go home. Returning emptyhanded—childless— was not an option. Hopefully Rain would come back to her senses when they found Lilly.

Ahead of him, the warriors approached a sharp turn. There were shouts of greeting as they intercepted another group, though a boulder blocked him from seeing the downhill travelers. James found a burst of speed and barged through the warriors, past the boulder, expecting to see—

"Lilly!"

A bunch of hippie women gazed at him. While the savages explained who he was, James rushed through the strangers with rude hands, pushing them aside, because maybe...

Maybe they'd cured Lilly and returned her to normal size. Maybe she was hiding behind one of their grungy dresses, waiting to jump out and surprise him.

"Lilly?" Now he was ahead of everyone on the trail. The pack of women stood below him, but Lilly wasn't there. "She isn't with you?" he pleaded.

The hippies shook their heads, confused. "No, you have to keep going."

"She's fine, as fine as can be." This one sounded like someone appraising a new ship, not the health of an imperiled girl.

"See you back home," called the flame-haired one as

they continued downward.

"We gotta talk about fixing that door," said Decembra on her way up.

James wanted to scream. Rip out his hair. Bash somebody's head against a rock until they told him—precisely—where to find his daughter. These women understood nothing about a father's anguish, and their casual manner made him doubt their intention. But the warriors were back on the march, heading over a low dip between the mountains.

He hurried to catch up before the last of them dropped out of sight.

Soon James found himself at the foot of a mountain that struck him, somehow, as *gentler*. That was the word it inspired. He would've described its color as soft, its vegetation as plucky, and its rocky formations as whimsical—or even childlike. A rabbit bounded across the path. That, too, bode well: it wasn't a wolf or a cougar or some other predator with which the warriors might feel a kinship. A raven circled above them and let out a foreign sound, an unarticulated squawk.

The procession stopped.

"We'll leave you now. It'll be easy from here." Decembra and the others turned homeward.

"Thank you!" Rain waved goodbye to her new comrades.

"Wait! Where's Lilly?" The panic came on again. This was no place to be left alone.

"If you can't find her now," said the girl who'd befriended Rain, "then you're truly blind."

They had the gall to laugh before they abandoned him.

"How will we find our way back?" James called.

"Don't worry Mr. Wolf," Rain said. "It should be pretty easy." She continued up the mountain, quick and light-footed, and utterly indifferent to his hesitation.

James couldn't figure out how—or why, or when, or where—he'd become the only one who had no idea what was going on. Rain was more like his elder here and he hated feeling so small, so incompetent. So unheeded.

"Lilly?" Rain cast her eyes to the mountain's top as she glided up the next switchback. Her question was inquisitive, a hopeful girl wondering "Are you there?"

James responded with a brasher "Lilly!" A demand to stop fooling around. Where was she? Hiding in a cave?

"Lilly!" A demand that she show herself. "Lilly!"

He chased after Rain, short of breath. The mountain had gradual slopes, easy to walk paths, but it was immense. From the vistas he peered out toward the rest of the range, hoping to spot signs of civilization, another town. Or maybe a castle—that would appeal to Lilly; he could imagine her journeying to a castle.

A kingdom for his princess.

That's it! At last it made a degree of sense. Lilly found herself in a fairytale world and was rescued by a prince. Thank goodness—someone who'd protect her. James felt better, and more confident, now that he had a logical clue about what he should look for. He scoured the surrounding landscape as he climbed, looking for the first signs of a kingdom across the way.

There! A glint, a flash of light…

LILLY

They were almost there. Lilly heard them calling her name. She felt them the instant they crossed onto the range and put the valley behind them. It made her giddy. They were coming!

She checked in with herself, and was pleased with what she found: a comfort unlike any she had ever known. There'd been moments when she was small, snuggled in bed, where she thought *I'm so comfortable I'm never going to move!* But ten minutes later she'd roll over and find a new position just as good. But now—here—she was content in a way that wouldn't have been possible in her former life. Content like a tree that outlived its human neighbors. Content like the wind that never tired and had endless places to go. Content like a beam of sunshine, always able to warm itself.

Rain clambered up the paths. Lilly couldn't speak to her as she once had, but she could tell Rain knew. Rain didn't need words.

"Be careful!" That was her dad, farther behind, warning as Rain's feet dashed faster and faster, making the most pleasant of vibrations.

Her dad hurried too, but she didn't like his antsy stomping.

Rain clambered onto her shoulder and stood there looking around. Lilly did her new version of a giggle. Rain responded by backtracking. But her dad kept ascending, passing Rain as she went down and he went up.

Lilly howled with laughter as her mortal father clambered onto her head. She wanted to ask Rain, "Does he look ridiculous, standing on my eyebrows?"

"Lil-ly!" His voice carried far and wide, since she was the tallest mountain. But that's when Lilly understood: he couldn't see her. He had no sense of her at all. He called again, as if she was out there somewhere, not directly beneath his feet.

Rain curled into a nook between Lilly's elbow and her baby's toes.

Her father's impatient footfalls raced over her ear, across her shoulder.

"Where are you going?" Rain asked as he half-ran, half-slid down Lilly's impressive arm.

"I see something! Over that peak!" He stumbled downward, racing to get away. When he reached her knee, he crossed over onto an adjoining plateau of rock. Lilly felt him moving farther and farther away. "Lilly! I'm coming!"

Where was he going? *Daddy, can't you see me?*

He wandered off course. His vibrations went silent. It made her sad. Soon she'd lose all awareness of him; he was on his own journey now.

"Hey," Rain whispered. "I can feel your heart."

Lilly returned to her happy state. There were many people who saw her and knew her for what she was, and she loved all of them.

"Is this your baby?" Rain asked. Lilly's daughter giggled as Rain tickled her heel. "I'm going to sit with you for a long, long time, okay? I'm so glad you came here. I made friends with Alala and maybe I can stay, or at least visit really often."

Lilly's heart purred in the way of the earth, deep in the rocks with their long memories. She was wrong before: *this* was utter contentment, with her daughter in her arms, and her best friend, nestled against her chest. She could hold them for eternity.

The endless nows.

The fleeting forevers.

ACKNOWLEDGEMENTS

This little book has a very special place in my heart and soul. Thank you to the early readers who fell in love with Lilly: Paula D'Alessandris, Christie LeBlanc, Claudie Wilson, John Stage, and Deborah Stage. Thank you to my agents, Claire Friedman and Stephen Barbara, for championing this project. And a giant-sized thank you to Steve Berman for sharing Lilly with the world.

ZOJE STAGE is the *USA Today* and internationally bestselling author of BABY TEETH, WONDERLAND, and GETAWAY. A former filmmaker with a penchant for the dark and suspenseful, she lives in Pittsburgh.

This body text is set in ATHELAS, a serif typeface designed by Veronika Burian and Jose Scaglione. Released by their company TypeTogether in 2008, Burian and Scaglione described ATHELAS as inspired by British fine book printing. It won joint first prize for best Latin-alphabet body text face at the Granshan International Type Design Competition in 2008 and is named after a healing herb in Tolkien's *The Lord of the Rings*.

The title and chapter headings are set in **ADAM CG PRO**, an all-caps, san-serif typeface designed by Shrenik Ganatra, inspired by Futura.

9 781590 215234